MW01049086

Coimirceoirí
Guardians of the Marked Ones

Book I: Journey to The Rift

by

Cathi Shaw

Ink Smith Publishing

www.ink-smith.com

Copyright © 2016 Cathi Shaw

All Rights Reserved

Journey to The Rift

Coimirceoirí: Guardians of the Marked Ones, Book 1

by Cathi Shaw

Cover Design: Chris Arlidge of Cheeky Monkey Media

Map by Caitlin Shaw

Author Photo by Becca McNeil

Formatted by: VJO Gardner

All rights reserved. This book or any portion thereof may not be reproduced or used in any manner whatsoever without the express written permission of the publisher except for the use of brief quotations in a book review.

The final approval for this literary material is granted by the author.

Printed in the U.S.A, 2016

All characters appearing in this work are fictitious. Any resemblance to real persons, living or dead is purely coincidental.

ISBN: 978-1-939156-87-7

Ink Smith Publishing

710 S. Myrtle Ave Suite 209

Monrovia, CA 91016

www.ink-smith.com

Acknowledgements

Thanks to all the readers of the Marked Ones series, who badgered me for more Five Corners adventures. I hope you enjoy this instalment of the prequel to the series.

Special thanks to my wonderful beta readers: Carol Doyle Jones and Tarie Lynn Rempel for enthusiastically reading the draft of this book and giving such honest and heartfelt feedback.

Thanks once again to my daughter, Cait, who continues to be my writing companion and muse for all my projects. This book wouldn't have been completed with her.

I am so very grateful to Meaghan Craven for her outstanding editing skills. I was thrilled to have such a gifted and generous editor work on this book.

Thank you to Chris Arlidge and Treena Bjarnson for making sure this instalment of The Marked Ones once again had a beautiful cover. Chris, your talents as an artist continue to astound me.

And special thanks to Ashley Howie and the team at Ink Smith, the best little publishing family one could ask for.

Dedication

To all the readers of The Marked Ones series, your continued excitement for this story inspires me every day.

Characters

Queen Aibhilín (AHV- i-leen – Elder queen of ancient times who sacrificed herself to the darkness
Aranel (Are-uh-nell) – Nurse to Prince Meldiron
Bellasiel (Bella-seel) – Elder healer
Beriadan (Bear-ee-ah-dahn) – Senior Elder knight
Brijit (Bri-jeet) Carnesîr – Chosen Coimirceoirí from the Academy
Elsa – Brijit's friend at the Academy
Eöl Ar-Feiniel (Ay-owl Are-Fen-el) – Elder and archivist
Erulassë (Air-oo-lahs-say) – Mother of Princess Neirdre and sister of Nestariel
Finn – Weylon's friend at Stone Mountain
Gregor – Weylon's mentor at Stone Mountain
Meldiron (Mel-dear-on) – Son of Princess Neirdre and Crown Prince Suiadan
Minathrial (Min-ath-ree-al) – Name chosen for future queen of the Elders
Mistress Cowan – Headmistress at the Academy
Nestariel (Nehs-tahr-ee-ell) – Elder healer and Mistress of Tèarmann
Princess Neirdre (NE-a-Dra) – Princess of the Elders
Raina (Rai-na) – Elder girl servant at Téarmann
Raspella – Brijit's mentor at the Academy, a potions instructor
Samred – Aranel's son
Serena – Brijit's friend at the Academy
Suiadan (Soo-ee-ah-dahn) – Crown Prince of the Elders
Weylon Forborrow – Chosen Coimirceoirí from Stone Mountain

Terminology

Aptrgangr (Aptr-ganga) – Forest creature or creatures that have been tainted by the evil from The Rift
Coimirceoir (Coym-eer-kee-oy-r) – Protector of the princess
Coimirceoirí (Coym-eer-kee-oy-ri) – Guardians of the Elders
Draíodóir (Dray-Or-Door) – Druid or Druids (magician or magicians)
Kurunii (Coo-roo-nee) – Witch or witches who live in Five Corners

Places

Bermgarten – Largest eastern city, where Serena is assigned duties
Dead Sea – A sea tainted by evil, to the west of Five Corners
Evendel – Village where Brijit grew up with her grandmother
Forbidden Coast – Western coastline that borders the Dead Sea
Island of Nasseet – Island to the south of Five Corners in the middle of the Sea of Arcadia
Jirgen Forest – Dying forest east of The Rift
Lowlands – Forested lands in the middle of Five Corners
Merryville – Small village east of the Academy
Outlands – Desert plains in the southwestern part of Five Corners
Pinefrest Mountains – in the North, where Elsa is assigned duties
Revuover – Large city close to the borders of Séreméla
Sailsburg – Southernmost port city in Five Corners
Sea of Arcadia – Sea to the south of Five Corners
Séreméla (Sar-A-Mell-A) – the Elders' home
Tèarmann (CHAR-mun) – Elder fortress on the edge of The Rift
The Rift – A little-known dead zone created to the west of Séreméla when Queen Aibhilín sacrificed herself to the Evil that was consuming the Dead Sea and threatening the rest of Five Corners
Wastelands – Land to the west of the Outlands, tainted by the Evil in The Rift; a place where no one lives and little grows
Western Sea – The name for the Dead Sea before it was tainted by the Evil

Prologue

"The Evil must be held back at all costs, my queen! We will fight to protect you!"

Aibhilín stood on the ramparts of the dark castle, her pale hair streaming behind her. She held back the emotions that were coursing through her. What her Captain of the Guard did not understand was that the Elders were not prepared to give up as much as he thought they would. "At all costs" was not something her people understood. Instead, they took and took and took. They didn't want to give up their lifestyle or comforts. She herself had been guilty of the same mentality until she had seen the devastation their excess was causing. Her people were selfish and foolish. In recent years, she had come to understand this. She knew she had done all she could in this realm to convince them to change their ways.

As she stared into the vast darkness in front of her, a sureness came over her. As the Elders' leader, it was up to her to break this cycle of destruction. She knew what she must do.

Her closest advisor objected when she told him her plan. "It will be a short remedy, Queen Aibhilín. What will happen when the magik wanes?"

Aibhilín was silent as her advisers began to argue in earnest. They were quite correct. This would be a short solution. But it would hold the Evil at bay for a time, until her people were ready to make the true sacrifice they must. Or until the Chosen One appeared and sealed the Evil for good.

Her guards shifted nervously behind her. The darkness in front of them churned with wickedness. It was a living thing. And while the option that was presented to them was not ideal, they had no choices left. They would act or they, and all of Five Corners, would perish.

"The Prophecy speaks of this," Aibhilín said finally. "This and what will happen in the future." Her tone was calm.

"But, Queen Aibhilín, your life will be shortened if you do this. The Darkness will bind you."

Her lips lifted in amusement. They were so naïve, the men who surrounded her. They had no idea that the Darkness had been with her from the beginning. And it had been calling her more and more lately. Every time she had used magik in the last three years, she had felt the tug of that darkness, inviting her to join it. She had helped to create this – as much if not more than most of them. No, she was not the one who would save Five Corners, but she could attempt to give her country time to heal and to begin to make the changes that were needed.

The Chosen One that the Prophecy named had not yet been born, would not be born for generations. But Aibhilín's job in this realm was done. Now she must bind to the darkness. Her essence would protect her people and all of Five Corners.

For a time.

She only hoped that amount time would be enough for her people to recognize that the world would not be healed through their greed and excess. They, too, would have to sacrifice or they would lose it all.

The arguments from the Elder council rose in volume. She let them bicker as she stared into the Darkness. Their arguments were weak. None of them wanted to make a true sacrifice. None of them wanted to give up their queen. The irony was that none of them even realized that they had contributed, and were still contributing, to this growing evil. It seemed as if she were the only one who had seen the truth.

As their leader, she felt her destiny was clear.

She raised her arms and they fell silent. "It is done," she said with certainty. And the tone of her voice brooked no argument.

The silence followed her as she made her way down to the plain. Her guards flanked her. A hundred feet out on the sands, she turned to them.

"I will not allow you to sacrifice yourselves. You will protect our homeland. You and your children will keep her safe. I will be with you always."

She saw the tears that glinted in the strong men's eyes and she smiled again, gently this time.

"This is how it has to be. Rest easy, my comrades."

And with those last words, the great Queen Aibhilín turned and walked into the darkness.

The guards and the members of the Elder council who were present that day saw what happened, but it was so unbelievable that the legend of her act, told for centuries afterward, was considered folklore rather than a true story.

As the Darkness greedily rushed to envelop Aibhilín, there was a flash of light so bright and hot it blinded those who were looking directly at it. After the flash, the queen was consumed by the dark; in a blink of the eye, she was gone. As the onlookers watched in disbelief, a magikal border rose up and the earth cracked in two. The Rift was born and Five Corners was saved.

For a time.

Chapter One

"Brijit! Wait for us!"

Brijit turned to see Serena and Elsa walking down the empty, brick-lined hallway behind her. The clicks of their boot heels on the polished marble floor echoed through the vacant hall as they scurried as quickly as they dared without breaking into a run. They looked ridiculous. One of the unspoken rules of the Academy was that students never run in the halls. Even the preteen girls who trained with them knew this. Eighteen-year-old soon-to-be graduates were expected to conduct themselves with grace at all times.

"Where are you going without us?" Serena scolded as she linked arms with Brijit. "Not looking for the Stone Mountain *Coimirceoirí* on your own, are you?" she teased.

Elsa giggled, and Brijit rolled her eyes.

"Hardly. I'm heading to Raspella's chambers."

"Oh, seriously, Brij? Why?" Elsa asked incredulously.

Brijit kept her face free of all expression. With the assignments being announced tonight, she did not want to discuss her growing unease with her friends. They wanted to celebrate and have a bit of fun. And she knew they would be in no mood to hear about her suspicions.

She pasted a smile on her face and pretended to be interested in their plans to hunt down some boys from Stone Mountain and start celebrating early. But Brijit wasn't so sure celebrating was in order. She couldn't shake the feeling that had been growing in her mind for the last few months. Something was being planned that the *Coimirceoirí* had no say in; something the Elders were in charge of, and she wasn't sure it was a good thing.

Serena stopped in her tracks when she recognized that Brijit's mind was elsewhere. "Please tell me you're not thinking about your conspiracy theories again?"

Brijit sighed. Okay, so she may have casually mentioned her worries to her friends more than once in the past few months. And, true, she had not yet been able to uncover anything concrete in her research, but she still had that niggling feeling that her grandmother had trained her to never ignore. After what she had witnessed in Merryville, she was even more convinced that something sinister was going on. Not that she'd told her friends about that. For some reason, she'd felt compelled to keep those events to herself…at least for now.

Of course, going with your hunches with no substantive evidence, or none that you could share, made it rather difficult to explain yourself even to your closest friends, especially when you weren't ready to talk about the true root of your concerns.

But Brijit felt her time to uncover this mystery was running out. Tonight their fates would be decided, and in the next few days they would be scattered across Five Corners. By that point it would be too late to convince Serena and Elsa that something was not right with what the Elders were doing. Brijit would feel much better knowing her best friends knew what she had discovered, and were on her side, should something happen.

The three of them had met soon after arriving at the Academy five years ago. At first glance they were an unlikely trio. Serena, a blond beauty, was easily the prettiest girl at the Academy. And Elsa, with her wit and kindness, was the most popular. Brijit, on the other hand, was the bookworm of their year and tended to question everything, which made her unpopular with some of their classmates and many of their teachers.

Still, the girls had bonded quickly when they had been assigned as roommates in their first year, and now they were as close as sisters. It was hard to imagine that the next few days would be their last ones together.

Brijit couldn't believe that their studies were finally coming to an end. After anticipating graduation and their assignments for so long, now everything seemed to be moving too fast to be real.

She knew that Elsa and Serena just wanted to cut loose and celebrate. And her friends weren't alone in wanting to do so – the halls were buzzing with other students anticipating the evening's festivities. But the graduation ceremony was only one part of why her classmates were so excited. Today was the day the *Coimirceoirí* students from Stone Mountain would make their first appearance at the Academy. The *male* students.

As was tradition, the younger girls would not be present when the Stone Mountain apprentices arrived. Although five years of students usually resided at the Academy, every year when the senior class graduated and the male students arrived, the younger girls were taken on a week of various field trips. The faculty pointed to tradition for this practice, but everyone knew it was to keep the younger, supposedly more impressionable, girls away from the older boys.

Brijit had pointed out the major flaw in that reasoning was that it did nothing to keep the older girls away from the male *Coimirceoirí*. And over the last few days, it seemed that most of the girls at the Academy could talk of nothing else. Even Serena and Elsa had been preoccupied.

Brijit had listened to her friends' excited chatter as they analyzed every detail of the coming meeting with the boys, the first they would have come across in their five years of training. She had to admit that she, too, was curious about the young men who would be arriving but probably not in the same way her friends were.

She'd seen her friends flirt endlessly with the boys they met in the village, but the simple, honest town boys were no match for the allure of the male *Coimirceoirí*. Brijit shook her head. For Elsa and Serena (and many of their fellow students) part of the excitement was knowing that they, as *Coimirceoirí*, were forbidden to marry. And while the Elders tended to turn a blind eye to relationships *Coimirceoirí* might have with the "regular" people of Five Corners, they strictly banned all relations between two *Coimirceoirí.*

The instructors at the Academy tried to scare them into accepting this rule by telling them the old legend of Ester and Kane. The story went that the two were matched as *Coimirceoirí* apprentices but that their bond went beyond the work they did for the Elders. They had fallen deeply in love. As a result, their attention had been so focused on one another that they failed to protect the royal family, including the small Crown Prince and his mother, who was rumored to have been carrying the next great heir to the Elder throne: the elusive girl-child.

Brijit didn't really believe the Elders could have known that that ancient princess had been carrying a girl, but it did make the story more powerful. As a result of Ester and Kane's neglect, the prince and his pregnant mother had been murdered. Lucky for the Elders there had been a younger prince safely stowed away in Séreméla who had been able to take on the role of Crown Prince after his older brother's demise.

The story of Ester and Kane reeked of fairytale to Brijit. But still, the Elders and the instructors had used it for hundreds of years to keep another *Coimirceoirí* couple from mating. And it had worked, like so many of the rules and regulations that were imposed upon them. They drove Brijit nuts.

The ban on marriage was ridiculous in Brijit's mind. Why couldn't they marry? It wasn't as if the ban really made the *Coimirceoirí* any less likely to have romantic affairs. They just had to be more discrete about them.

It was obvious to her that if some of the old traditions were changed, all this silliness would be eliminated. It was a waste of their time and energy. Part of Brijit wondered if the traditions were kept so the flirtations continued. After all, indiscretions acted as distractions that kept the *Coimirceoirí* from questioning other rules the Elders held too dearly.

It would be a simple matter to cull the appeal of the male students. All they had to do was to let the girls and boys train together. The fact that the Academy was an all-girls' school and Stone Mountain was an all-boys' school was more than half the problem. But the Elders insisted that their *Coimirceoirí* be trained the way they always had. As with many of the Elders' rules, it had no basis in logic. Almost no one questioned the Elders' ways, and it was more than enough to set Brijit's teeth on edge. She knew the she couldn't be the only one in Five Corners who disagreed with their outdated beliefs but few spoke out against the Elders, especially in public.

In her second year, when she'd first heard of Stone Mountain, Brijit had quizzed the headmistress about why only male students were allowed to train there. Her mentor, Raspella, had always seemed to agree with Brijit's rants about Stone Mountain, but it had been clear that she didn't have the power to do anything about it. So fourteen-year-old Brijit had approached Mistress Cowan. She had been told that the male and female students were trained in different settings for practical reasons. When she pushed the matter, Mistress Cowan had told her that her questioning nature was very valuable but she needed to stop challenging tradition. She had said there were more important things for Brijit to focus on. This would soon become the standard reply Brijit was given whenever she questioned the Elders' traditions or authority.

Of course, Brijit would be lying if she didn't admit that she was slightly intrigued by the male *Coimirceoirí*. Stone Mountain was far to the south along the Forbidden Coast, past the Outlands. Few knew much about the area, but folklore told of monsters and storms that raged so darkly that most of Five Corners considered it utterly uninhabitable. There were even some regular folks in the Five Corners who believed that Stone Mountain didn't truly exist. But the *Coimirceoirí* had been training their male students there for centuries. To survive the climate there alone would be a test of the students' strength. Brijit wanted to get one of the Stone Mountain

Coimirceoirí alone, but not for the reasons her peers might think – she simply wanted to discover what it was like to live in that part of Five Corners.

Serena and Elsa were giggling about the few male *Coimirceoirí* they had managed to spot when the Stone Mountain delegation had arrived the previous evening. Of course, the girls had been sneaking around the Academy's halls after curfew. Brijit had stayed in their room, engrossed in an old scroll she'd found in the library that afternoon, which traced the ancestry of the Elders back to Queen Aibhilín. She had barely noticed when they returned from their spying mission.

"Aren't you even a little bit curious as to where we will be assigned?" Brijit asked, trying to bring her friends thoughts back to more practical matters.

Serena rolled her eyes. "It's obvious you will be the one who is selected this year, Brijit. None of the rest of us are even close in ability."

Elsa nodded in agreement. "We've accepted the futility of it all since Year One."

"And we will be sent where we are sent. There is no point fretting about it," Serena added. "It will be announced tonight, whether we worry about it or not."

Brijit stifled a sigh. Each year, when the senior group of students graduated to begin their work with the Elders, two of their ranks were chosen to fulfill their practicums at the palace in Séreméla. The best male and best female of each class were chosen as apprentices to the royal family.

While she appreciated her friends' confidence, and she hoped they were right, she didn't dare jinx herself by believing it. Brijit's skills were in healing and as an empath. Her skills in the latter area had caught the most attention in her years at the Academy. Brijit's mentor Raspella had worked hard to help Brijit hone her empathic skills, which were now not only better than the rest of her classmates' but also better than those of her instructors.

Despite her many gifts as a *Coimirceoirí*, however, Brijit's outspoken and questioning manner might count against her when the Elders chose the palace apprentices. While Raspella had appreciated her assertive nature, Brijit knew many of the instructors at the Academy did not. And she doubted the Elders would want such a difficult student to join them in Séreméla. They preferred *Coimirceoirí* apprentices to be obedient servants. An inquisitive, questioning one would not be welcome.

Of course, the female apprentice they chose to go to Séreméla would, in large part, depend on who the male apprentice was and what his talents might be. Brijit felt a prick of irritation. She hated to think her fate might hinge on what some unknown male student's skills were.

Her attention was drawn back to her friends, who were watching her expectantly.

"What?" Brijit asked, realizing with a flush of guilt that that she had been lost in her thoughts and not listening to their conversation at all.

"I said you're not going to spend the whole afternoon with Raspella going over tinctures you could make in your sleep, are you?"

Brijit bit her lip. She would prefer if they believed that was what she intended to do. She knew they would insist on coming with her if they knew her real plans. She didn't want them or anyone else to know what she was up to, yet. And not just because the Elders and Academy instructors would be livid if they found out but also because she didn't want her friends to get into trouble just as they were preparing for graduation. It would be better if they flirted with the male *Coimirceoirí* than accompany Brijit on her afternoon activities. The less they knew, the safer they would be.

Serena stared at her hard before raising her eyebrows in disbelief. "They've already made the decision about who will be going to Séreméla, Brij. There's no point in trying to impress them anymore."

Brijit pressed her lips together and didn't reply.

Elsa shook her head. "Never mind, Serena, she's a lost cause. Brijit, you do know that our freedom is coming to an end?"

Serena sighed in disappointment. "We *will* see you tonight, right?"

"Of course," Brijit nodded. She watched as her friends walked down the corridor ignoring the pang of guilt she felt for not joining them.

Freedom. What her friends didn't understand was that Brijit had accepted that her freedom was over the moment she had agreed to train as a *Coimirceoirí*. The honor had been too great for her to refuse, not that she'd even considered refusing (much to Grandmamma's disappointment). Brijit had wanted more than anything to serve the Elders in this way. It had been her ambition from a young age to help Five Corners in any way she could. She shook her head now, unable to believe just how naïve she had been.

Ever since she had been a young girl, it had been clear that Brijit had inherited her grandmother's skill as a healer. But Brijit wanted so much more than what her grandmother had settled for. While being the wise woman in the village was an honor on a local level, it was not what Brijit craved. She wanted, more than anything, to make a real difference in the world. She knew she could do just that as a *Coimirceoirí*.

She wanted to be the Academy's apprentice, not just for the honor of it. If Brijit's hunch was right, what was happening in Five Corners centered on what was going on in Séreméla. She needed to be placed there if she wanted to get to the bottom of the mystery. But there was no point in fretting about that. She couldn't control the decision that had already been made. Instead, she would make the best of her remaining time at the Academy and see what she could find out – even if it meant leaving her principles in the closet for now.

#

As Brijit entered the laboratory, the pungent odor of multiple herbs and tinctures flooded her senses. The room was empty, exactly as she expected it to be.

Brijit had no intention of meeting with Raspella. She had tried to ask questions of her mentor too many times over the last few months, ever since that trip to Merryville. She closed her eyes briefly as the memories assaulted her again.

The small dirty girl dressed in rags who had grabbed at her hand as Brijit followed Raspella through the village.

"Please, tell me why," the girl sobbed.

Brijit did not understand what she was saying and had to gently shake off the girl as she hurried to catch up with her mentor. Raspella was marching into the tiny town hall where the council of the small village was gathered. In front of them was a dead child, no more than five years old. Brijit was shocked. The child had clearly been murdered, and it appeared the deed had been done at the hands of the villagers themselves.

"Is this the first one?" Raspella asked the mayor.

He nodded, his face grim.

Raspella stared at the body for a moment. "Show me."

The wise woman of the village turned the child's body over and pulled the ragged dress on her shoulder down to reveal a black mark. Brijit stared at it. She had seen that symbol before.

"You have done the right thing," Raspella told the villagers. "Burn the body."

And with that. her mentor motioned to Brijit and they left. Brijit waited for Raspella to tell her what it meant, but her mentor remained silent on the journey home. They had not planned on visiting that particular village that day – they had been on business in another town not far away where Brijit had helped to deliver a baby as one of her final healing tests. The summons to Merryville had been last minute, and Raspella had clearly not been happy about having to take Brijit with her but she also had been told that she could not delay.

It was only when they returned to the Academy that Raspella turned to Brijit and said, "I trust you will not tell anyone what you saw." Her mentor looked at her sternly.

"What did I see?" Brijit asked tersely, still unable to believe how coldly Raspella had acted in the presence of a murdered innocent.

"Nothing that you need to worry about."

Brijit couldn't believe her ears. "A village murders a child because of a mark on her shoulder and I'm not to worry about it?" It was unthinkable not only that the Academy would condone such behavior but that they would hide it.

Raspella stopped her tracks outside the gates to the Academy and gripped Brijit's shoulders hard. "You will not speak of this, Brijit Carnesîr. I can't explain what you saw but I will tell you that everything that was done happened on Elders' orders." Her mentor's words hit her like a slap. Raspella following Elders' orders so closely was unheard of.

Inside the laboratory now, Brijit felt outrage rising in her chest again. The Elders seemed to control everything, no questions asked. Raspella was one of few people at the Academy who had no problem critiquing the Elders. But for some reason she was now blindly following their orders. Brijit had not pushed Raspella on the matter. Something in her mentor's demeanor had warned her to keep her mouth shut. But she had not forgotten what she had seen. Nor had she told her mentor that she'd seen that symbol before…in fact that she wore it every day around her neck.

Brijit reached inside her dress and felt the pewter pendant hanging there. Her grandmother had given her that pendant before she left home and told her to always keep it out of sight but on her person. Brijit had thought nothing of it. She assumed it was just a family heirloom that her grandmother had wanted her to have. Now she wasn't so sure.

Looking around the laboratory again to make sure she was quite alone, Brijit pulled the pendant out and gazed at it. The triquetra inside a circle was exactly the same as the mark she'd seen on the dead child's shoulder. What it meant was a mystery to her.

Frowning, she slipped the chain back beneath her gown and made her way across the room to Raspella's office. For months now she'd been trying to get answers about what had happened in Merryville. And for months she'd found nothing. Even the Academy library seemed to be missing information related to the rune that was on her chain. Other symbols were listed in the books, but that particular one was not there.

And two weeks ago the dreams had suddenly started. Brijit didn't know what they meant, but she'd been waking feeling panicky and anxious, her sheets twisted and soaked in sweat. The dreams were not exactly the same but similar in content. Her grandmother kept popping into them to warn her that she was in grave danger. The rune was always floating in the background of a charred and inhospitable landscape that was ravaged and churning with a darkness so evil it left her heart pounding when she woke.

Other themes cropped up in the dreams, too. Dead children with the black triquetra burned into their shoulders, even babies with the mark. Elders laughing behind closed doors. But none of it made sense to her. Brijit might have been able to forget what had happened in the village, but her dreams reinforced her feeling that something was going on. She didn't know what it was, but her gut told her it was something sinister.

Brijit had the distinct impression that Raspella knew more than she was willing to share. The commands may have come from the Elders, but her mentor was definitely involved in the specifics of what was happening.

Looking behind her once more to make sure the lab was empty, Brijit tried the door to Raspella's office and was mildly surprised to find it unlocked. The potions instructor was notorious for locking her door and enforcing what little privacy she had as an instructor at the Academy. It was out of character for her to forget this one detail, particularly when she was not in the lab teaching.

Rather than question this good luck, Brijit pushed the door open and let herself into the office. Closing the door behind her, she squinted in the darkness and then fumbled in her pocket for the candle she'd brought with her. Swiftly lighting it, she set it on Raspella's cluttered desk and began sifting through the papers that covered every inch of the space.

Her mentor was never a tidy person. Her desk was covered with ungraded assignments and fragments of potions, along with random ingredients. Shaking her head, Brijit shuffled the papers around until she saw a letter haphazardly stuffed between two first-year papers. Scanning the contents Brijit suddenly gasped when she saw her own name spelled out in Elder script. Lowering herself to Raspella's chair behind the desk, Brijit focused on translating the Elder language.

Brijit Carnesîr is our selected apprentice this graduating class.

Brijit stopped reading as a rush of pride filled her. She was actually going to Sérémela! She had done it. A smile pulled at her lips. Then she continued reading.

We have reviewed the concerns stated by yourself and the other instructors at the Academy but the Crown Prince and the Council insist that her gifts far outweigh her spirited nature. We are confident that we will be able to control her.

Pain stabbed at her as the meaning of those words sunk in. Brijit's smile faded. Raspella must have argued against her nomination as the apprentice for this year. But why? She had thought her mentor was on her side, but this letter suggested the Elders were the ones who wanted her. Even if they said they would have to control her. Brijit snorted at that. The Elders were arrogant enough to assume they could control all *Coimirceoirí*. Well, they were about to be surprised if they thought they could control her.

The next lines in the letter also caught her attention.

As you know, this year's apprentices will not be going to Séreméla but will be taken to The Rift.

Brijit paused in her reading, her brow furrowed. What was The Rift? She had never heard of apprentices not going to Séreméla. Elders valued tradition over all else. Something had to be very wrong for them to change this tradition so radically. Her gaze returned to the letter.

The Coimirceoirí's job there is urgent. Brijit, in particular, is needed by the Royal family. The time of the Prophecy is approaching, and her skill will be necessary in coming days.

Brijit ran her hand through her hair. What skills were they referring to? Her healing skills? Surely not. The Elders themselves were renowned healers. So did they mean her empathetic skill set? But that didn't really make sense either. And what was the Prophecy? She had never heard of it. And where was The Rift? As far as she knew, such a place did not exist in Five Corners.

Brijit raced through the rest of the letter, looking for more clues, but the remaining paragraph only included the usual niceties of polite conversation and a signature line. Frowning, she carefully put the letter back between the two assignments where she had found it.

She scanned Raspella's desk, looking for more clues. Surprisingly, she didn't have to look hard. Buried under a stash of dried lavender and wax candles, she found a map of Five Corners that she had never seen before. Squinting, Brijit brought it closer to the candle and gasped. Where traditional maps only showed Séreméla and the open Sea of Arcadia, this map had another section labeled The Rift. In fact, the entire western part of Five Corners appeared to be rewritten. Chewing on her lip, Brijit considered her options. She could attempt to sketch what she saw on the map, but she was hopeless at drawing and she had no materials with her anyway. The details on this map were intricate. She could try to commit it to memory, but she didn't trust herself.

Then a thought occurred to her. She would be leaving the Academy in the next few days. She now knew she was one of the Elders' apprentices for this year. The Elders usually collected their *Coimirceoirí* apprentices within two days of the banquet. Classes weren't set to resume for the younger students for another week. Chances were good that Raspella would not be in her office before Brijit left. Or if she was, she wouldn't notice the map missing until it was too late.

Ignoring the stab of guilt that assaulted her for taking what was not hers, Brijit stuffed the map into her bag and then looked around Raspella's desk to see if there were any other clues. Everything else appeared to be things the potions instruction would normally be working on.

Sighing, Brijit searched the bookshelves but saw nothing related to either the Prophecy the letter mentioned or the rune she'd seen on the dead child's shoulder. Admitting defeat, she straightened and looked around the room once more, making sure everything was as she had found it. Then she blew out her candle and slipped out the door. She may not have found the answers she was hoping for, but she certainly had more information than when she'd arrived. The only problem was the things she had discovered left her with more questions than answers.

#

Brijit returned to her rooms with barely enough time to change into her formal Academy graduation robes. She was surprised when she saw that neither Elsa nor Serena were there yet. She had expected her friends to be in the midst of primping for the ceremony. She took advantage of their absence to tuck the map into her traveling bags which she had already started to prepare for her trip. Although she hadn't known that she would be the Academy apprentice this year, all the *Coimirceoirí* graduates would be leaving the school within the next week so most of the girls had started to pack up their things.

She straightened and looked over to Serena's and Elsa's beds, where their robes were neatly laid out. It didn't make sense that they weren't here. All the graduates were required to wear their graduation dress robes, but she expected most of the girls would be taking extra time with their hair and accessories in an attempt to impress the male students. Judging by how excited her friends had been this morning, she had assumed they would be especially diligent with their appearance.

Brijit frowned as she ran a brush through her short hair. They clearly hadn't returned from their earlier adventures. She wondered if they had met up with a couple of the male *Coimirceoirí* and lost track of time. She wouldn't put it past them.

But, no, it didn't make sense that Serena would miss the banquet. As much as everyone focused on her looks, Brijit knew her friend was keen to discover if she would be stationed in Bermgarten as she hoped. It was one of the largest cities in Five Corners, and Serena had announced her plans to be placed there midway through their second year together.

"I come from one of the tiniest villages in the country, Brijit. Can you imagine what an honor it would be to be stationed in the largest eastern city?"

And Brijit believed that her friend had a very good chance of being so placed. She was the most promising healer of their year. And everyone knew that Bermgarten valued apprentices who were healers beyond all else.

Serena would be back in time for the ceremony; Brijit was sure of it. And so would Elsa, even if it was only to see where everyone ended up. Elsa was the one girl in their year who liked to know what was going on with everyone. She wouldn't miss hearing each girl's station announced.

No, it was very odd that they were cutting it so close to the ceremony time. Brijit frowned. A shiver of fear ran down her spine. She hoped nothing had happened to the girls.

Shaking her head, she put her brush down and bent to lace up her shoes. She was letting what she'd discovered in Raspella's office taint her thoughts. Regardless of what the letter and the map might suggest, it didn't mean that all of the Academy was corrupt. And there was no reason to think her friends might be in danger. More likely they were still flirting with the boys.

No, Serena and Elsa had nothing to worry about. In fact, Brijit was the one who seemed to have less than loyal instructors at the Academy. Anger began to bubble in her stomach as she remembered what she had read in the letter. Even after what had happened in Merryville, she had thought Raspella was her ally. Clearly, however, she had not wanted Brijit to be chosen as the Academy's apprentice.

Before Brijit could completely tamp down her anger, the door banged open. Serena and Elsa burst into the room, immediately ripping her thoughts away from her deceitful mentor. Her friends were clearly upset. Serena's blond curls were escaping from her neat braid, and Elsa's cheeks were flushed.

Brijit stood up in alarm when she saw the raw fear on Elsa's face.

"Elsa? What happened?"

Serena closed the door and turned to Brijit, her turquoise eyes shining with tears.

Brijit's heart began to pound. "What's going on?"

Serena pushed Elsa toward her bed. "We need to act as if all is fine, Elsa. Get dressed for the banquet." Serena was pulling her day clothes off as she spoke. She paused to wipe the tears from her eyes.

"Serena, what happened?" Brijit said more sternly.

She looked at Brijit and shook her head. "You were right to be suspicious, Brijit. Something is going on, and it's worse than any of us imagined."

Chapter Two

As they dressed, the girls explained what had happened. They had gone looking for the boys from Stone Mountain as they said they were going to do. But they had been sidetracked after only seeing a few of them in the distance on the training field.

Elsa had come up with the idea of taking a shortcut through the northern dorms in an effort to get a better look at the boys down on the field, and that's when they had almost stumbled upon a secret meeting.

"We didn't think anything of it," Serena said shakily. "We just dove into the nearest wardrobe and took cover, waiting for whoever it was to move along."

Only they hadn't moved on. Instead they'd had a lengthy meeting in what was supposed to an empty dormitory. The second years who normally resided there were on the week-long field trip. It didn't take long before Serena and Elsa realized that it was a meeting that they shouldn't have been an audience to.

"Who was it?" Brijit asked.

"Mistress Cowan, the headmaster of Stone Mountain Academy, one of their senior instructors and…" Elsa paused and looked at Serena before adding, "Raspella."

"Did they discover you?"

Elsa shook her head. "No, but it was close."

"Too close," Serena let out a shaky breath. "If they knew we were there I don't know if we would have ever been allowed to leave given what we overheard."

Brijit was surprised. What could the girls have overheard that put them in such danger?

"Brijit, you are the female chosen to serve as Séreméla apprentice this year."

"I know," Brijit admitted with a frown.

Elsa looked at her sharply.

"I found some correspondence in Raspella's room that outlined the details of my assignment. Although it didn't really make much sense."

"That's because you're not going to Séreméla," Serena told her seriously. "Brijit, I fear you're in grave danger."

"What exactly did you overhear, Serena?"

Her friend looked at the clock on the wall and shook her head. "We can't be late. Not tonight. It would draw unwanted attention our way. We'll talk after the ceremony, I promise. Then, maybe, between the three of us we can make some sense of all of this."

Brijit didn't like to leave it but when she looked at the clock and saw how late it already was, she knew Serena was right. They would have to discuss what they'd discovered after the graduation ceremony.

#

Weylon surveyed the convocation hall, letting his senses attune to the different emotions running through the novices and teachers filling the space. He wrinkled his nose. There were far too many giddy girls present for his liking. He wondered if any of the females in the room took the role of *Coimirceoirí* seriously. From what he could tell, it certainly didn't appear so.

Regardless, he would be stuck with one of them when he went to Séreméla. The thought did nothing to lighten his mood. He wasn't interested in supervising some silly female novice. Oh, technically he knew he wouldn't be supervising her, but what he'd seen since they'd arrived at the school the previous evening made him think that he'd have a lot of work on his hands at the palace. The male students were constantly running into groups of girls staring at them. It was pathetic.

"Wipe that grimace off your face or you'll have all of them running the other way!"

Weylon looked up from his dark musings to see his old friend, Finn, laughing at him.

"Well, come on, Weylon, look at all the lovelies! And to think we will each be assigned one of them." Finn grinned with appreciation.

"*Coimirceoirí* aren't to become involved with –"

Before he could finish his sentence, Finn interrupted. "Ah, now, technically I believe the rules states that *Coimirceoirí* aren't to marry anyone. Doesn't mean we can't have a bit of fun, now, does it?"

Weylon studied the table in front of him. Finn didn't take his commitments seriously, which ironically meant he would be in no danger of breaking the *Coimirceoirí* code forbidding marriage.

"Weylon, even the Elders don't expect us to be all work all the time. You need to loosen up." His friend shook his head. "I would think you'd be celebrating, after all tonight it will become official that you'll be off to Séreméla."

Weylon grunted but said nothing. Finn was unperturbed. He was used to Weylon's moods. The truth was, Weylon would rather have skipped this party and got on with his assignment. There was no question that he would be the male apprentice going to Séreméla. No one in his year was even close to matching him in combat, defense and strategy skills. In addition, his ability to sense power and deceit meant he was one of the top students in the last fifty years. That he had to be shackled to one of these girls was grating.

He'd even argued with his mentor that the old tradition be dropped. But Gregor refused to discuss such an idea.

"Do you have any idea what the Elders would say if they could hear you, Weylon?" his mentor had asked with a shake of his white head. "I admit you are talented, but you need to learn a bit of humility. In Séreméla they won't take kindly to your attitude."

Weylon had not replied. He thought a lot of the old traditions were merely the Elders' way of controlling the masses. And he resented their superiority. A fact that he'd not attempted to hide, even though his mentor told him it would get him in trouble.

"You may be the most gifted *Coimirceoirí* student in the last half-century," Gregor acknowledged, "but your attitude will be your downfall. Don't discount the female who will accompany you to Séreméla. You aren't invincible, and you do have your weaknesses."

Weylon conceded that he wasn't perfect, but from the look of the girls in this room, he doubted there was anyone who was even close to his match in skill. He scanned his fellow students and noticed how the male Coimirceoirí students were readily flirting with the females. It was ridiculous. They weren't here to become friends with the girls.

As his gaze passed over the giggling masses of girls, he was drawn to one. At first he hadn't even noticed her; she was so understated. She wore the same formal graduation robes as all the other females, but she had done nothing to make herself stand out from the crowd. While the others had primped, putting their hair in elaborate styles and painting their faces, her face was clean and her brown hair hung in soft waves to just below her ears. The short style highlighted her large eyes, which were clearly grey even from this distance. She was watching the room with an expression of nerves and concern. He wondered if she was one of the candidates to be chosen from the Academy this year. He had to admit she was very pretty, although she did nothing to enhance her natural beauty. Not that she should, he reminded himself. As a *Coimirceoirí* student, her focus should be on other things. But looking at the abundant use of face paint and hair dressings on the other girls in the room, it was clear that most of the girls were focused on their male counterparts rather than their duties.

"I wonder what she's like," Finn's words interrupted Weylon's musings. He looked at his friend and was surprised to find him also watching the understated female *Coimirceoirí* he had noticed. She wasn't the type Finn usually went for. But then his friend went on, "Look at that hair!" and Weylon saw the tall, and indisputably beautiful girl with piles of blond waves standing at the elbow of the one who had attracted his own attention. On the other side of her was a very pretty dark-haired girl who seemed to be watching everyone at once with a look just short of terror on her face. He wondered why all three girls looked so distressed. Clearly, they weren't in the same mood as their classmates, who continued to whisper excitedly in the background.

Before he could reflect further on the girl in the corner, or her friends, the teachers were gathering on the dais and calling for the attention of the room.

Almost against his will, he looked back to where the brown-haired girl and her friends had been standing, but they had vanished.

#

"Stop looking so worried, Elsa!" Serena hissed under her breath. "We don't want to draw any unwanted attention."

"Too late for that," Elsa moaned.

Brijit looked at her in surprise and then glanced suspiciously around the ballroom to see if the instructors were watching them. But on the dais, Raspella, her red-haired instructor, was laughing with an instructor from Stone Mountain, a tall steely haired man. She didn't even glance in Brijit's direction.

"What do you mean?"

"Weylon Forborrow has already noticed us," Elsa whispered.

Brijit watched as the teachers finished organizing the scrolls on the table to the side of the dais. But Serena's words captured her full attention. She looked at her friend. "Who?"

"Weylon Forborrow is the most talented *Coimirceoirí* student in the last hundred years, or so some say."

Brijit was surprised. This was the first she'd heard of such a talented male student. Was it a coincidence that such a *Coimirceoirí* might exist this year?

"Last fifty years, Serena, quit exaggerating everything," Elsa scolded, then she tilted her head sideways. "The brooding one leaning on the pillar. Don't look now; he'll notice."

Ignoring her, Brijit looked across the room and saw a handsome, powerfully build young man watching the commotion at the front of the room with an expression of boredom and a hint of something else. She studied him for a few moments, trying to identify what it was. Suspicion, that's was it. His eyes were flitting about the hall too quickly, as if he were looking for something. Or someone. Instinctively she pulled her friends to the side behind a pillar.

"He's already been told he's going to Séreméla," Serena confided. "He's just waiting to see who will go with him."

Brijit raised her eyebrows in surprise. Novices were rarely told ahead of time of their assignments. For the others to know that he had been assigned to Séreméla early was telling. The instructors could have only one motive in revealing such information to the students: they wanted the rest of them to know they had an exceptional student in their class. But why would they want to spread such knowledge? It was out of character for them to share something like this with the students. Suspicion tickled her mind.

Brijit looked at Weylon Forborrow again, trying to see what she was missing, but he looked like any other male *Coimirceoirí*, granted a very handsome student, but not so very special.

"He's that talented?" she mused, disbelief coloring her words.

"I wonder if he's as cranky as he appears. No one will envy you if he is, Brijit!" Elsa said.

Brijit had to agree. He had what should have been a friendly face except it was marred with a scowl that made him wholly unapproachable.

Before they could speculate further, a tinkling bell rang, announcing the start of the formalities. The hall, buzzing with excitement only seconds earlier, became completely silent almost instantly.

The diminutive Mistress Cowan stepped forward and smiled at the students assembled. Brijit studied her, remembering that she had been part of the meeting her friends had inadvertently stumbled upon. Brijit wondered how much the headmistress knew about her assignment. She couldn't help wondering if Mistress Cowan had argued in her favor or not. And was it possible that she knew about the dead child in the village, too? It seemed likely. Brijit didn't think Raspella would be acting without Mistress Cowan's knowledge.

Mistress Cowan opened her mouth to speak but before she could utter a word, the doors to the convocation hall suddenly crashed open. Startled, Brijit and everyone in the hall turned. In the doorway three Elder knights were silhouetted. Her stomach dropped. As one, they stepped inside. All three were dressed in full armor. She had never seen Elders in full armor before. The sight was daunting. She saw that one had a huge broadsword strapped to his back while another had an Elder crossbow. They were dressed for battle. Fear began to creep up her spine.

Mistress Cowan spoke from the dais, "Beriadan, what is the meaning of this?"

"Our apologies for the interruption," the tallest Elder said in a tone that was anything but apologetic. "We are here for our new *Coimirceoirí.*"

The instructors on the dais rose in unison, their voices raised in protest.

"We have not officially announced the *Coimirceoirí* assigned to Séreméla yet," a wizened instructor from Stone Mountain said with disapproval.

"We have no time for that," Beriadan responded coolly, as his two companions began fanning through the crowded hall. One was striding right for her. The next words out of Beriadan's mouth were no surprise to her. "Brijit Carnesîr and Weylon Forborrow. Come."

And without a moment to say goodbye, Brijit found herself being led from the great hall, confusion warring with disbelief. She needed to speak to her friends. They couldn't just take her. But before she could digest what had just happened, Beriadan looked at her and spoke, confirming her fears. "We leave now."

Chapter Three

Despite his commanding manner, Beriadan was wrong about them leaving immediately, much to Brijit's relief. Mistress Cowan had quickly shown why she was in charge of all *Coimirceoirí* students. Brijit fought a smile as the tiny woman had stormed after the Elder knights and stopped them just outside the convocation hall.

She gave them a talking down loud enough for everyone in the vicinity to hear. Brijit had never heard anyone speak to Elders like that. And despite her anger with the Academy and what she had discovered, Brijit felt a wave of newfound respect for Mistress Cowan. With what she knew about Elders and the way they treated *Coimirceoirí*, Brijit was surprised when the headmistress's tongue lashing worked. In the end, Beriadan conceded to give them the night to prepare for the journey.

Brijit was redirected to her rooms and instructed to pack quickly. She hoped to get Serena and Elsa alone there, but her friends were detained in the convocation hall. Apparently the rest of the graduates were still being given their assignments. Frustration bubbled up inside her, but she forced herself to focus on the task at hand, knowing her friends would return to their rooms eventually.

Brijit had just finished sorting what little clothing she could take on the trip when Raspella arrived in her rooms under the pretense of helping her pack. After what she had discovered in her mentor's office, and her reluctance to speak about the dead child, Brijit didn't trust her one bit. She wondered what her real motives were for coming to her room, and Brijit was tempted to question the older woman but she held her tongue. Brijit didn't want to give away what she had discovered, and she was worried that if she got into an argument with Raspella, she might forget herself and mention what she had found. She knew Raspella would not approve of Brijit reading her personal correspondence and there was no possible reason Brijit could give for having searched her desk. So Brijit kept her mouth shut.

To her surprise, she found she didn't have to talk. Raspella was so livid about the change in plans and the way the Elders had taken over the ceremony that she bubbled over with complaints. For years, the superior attitude the Elders held with respect to the *Coimirceoirí* had been a sore topic for her mentor.

While Raspella had not been a chosen apprentice, her older brother had been. Or he had been until his early death. The Elders had not even returned his body to the family, a common practice, according to Raspella. She said they didn't respect the *Coimirceoirí* enough to even return their dead. It was just one of many faults her instructor had listed when it came to the Elders. This was why her seeming obedience to the Elders had bothered Brijit so much after their return from Merryville. She thought Raspella would have been eager to share what she knew with her star student, but that had not been the case. At the time, Brijit had wondered if her mentor's distaste for the Elders was just a show that she put on for the students. But if it was an act, she never seemed to fall out of character – except that one time.

Raspella continued to fume that the Elders were grandstanding to show their control over the students. She told Brijit that the other instructors were similarly outraged, but Brijit doubted any were as angry as Raspella.

While the Elders had agreed not to leave immediately, they had insisted that the chosen apprentices be ready to leave at dawn. Then they had disappeared to find their own shelter for the night.

After Raspella vented enough to regain her usual composure, she smiled at Brijit.

"Are you excited, my dear?" she asked.

Brijit swallowed and looked at her mentor. The quick change in her mood was a bit disconcerting. She automatically shielded herself from Raspella, not caring if her mentor noticed. Brijit didn't trust herself to keep her emotions hidden when the older woman was so clearly putting on an act. Brijit remembered the letter she had read, remembering that Raspella had spoken against her being sent to Séreméla. Brijit wondered if she would ever uncover the potion instructor's real motives. The fact that her mentor would argue against Brijit being chosen was more than just insulting. It was surprising.

It was a great honor to have one of your own students picked as the Academy apprentice. In fact, Raspella had never had one of her own make the cut before. A potions instructor rarely had a student as gifted as Brijit or, if they were, they were not typically seen as useful to the Elders.

Brijit looked at Raspella, who was watching her closely. For five years she had been like a mother to her. Her red hair, streaked with silver, hung in luscious curls midway down her back. Her brown eyes seemed to be full of love. Her unlined face looked like it always did: innocent and kind. Part of Brijit wanted to believe that Raspella had her best interests at heart, but she couldn't help remembering how her mentor had behaved in the last few months.

Brijit's distrust deepened. How long had Raspella argued against her being selected to go to Séreméla? Had she been against her from the start? How many lies had Raspella told her over the years?

Anger filled Brijit again, but she swallowed it back. Deceit was deep in the Academy. She had known that for years now. She had foolishly believed that Raspella was innocent and unaware of it all. This was her own fault for being naïve.

It was in her best interest now to push her emotions down and play along with whatever game Raspella was orchestrating. She only had a limited amount of time left to get information from her instructor. And the best way to do that was by playing dumb. She couldn't let them know that she was onto the illusion they so desperately wanted her to take as the truth. She could attempt to unravel how deep that illusion went later. For now, she had to try to get as much information as she could.

She focused on Raspella's earlier question. "Am I excited? I'm not sure if excited is quite the right word," she said carefully. "I am pleased."

That seemed to satisfy the older woman. Brijit continued to fold her clothes as Raspella continued to watch her closely. She doubled the energy she was using to shield herself from the older woman, ignoring the prodding sensation she always felt when someone with power tried to break through her shield. After a few more moments, however, the prodding stopped, and Raspella nodded in satisfaction.

Brijit was surprised. Her instructor seemed almost pleased that she had blocked her. Why? Raspella had to know that she was shielding herself. When one put up such a strong shield not only were one's feelings inaccessible to anyone who prodded, but one became like a blank slate. Those trained in probing others (as all instructors at the Academy were) would sense when someone was shielding themselves. So Raspella's next words surprised Brijit.

"I'm very proud of you, my dear." Her mentor's eyes glinted with some unreadable emotion. Before Brijit could decipher it, Raspella held out a small bag. "I've brought this for you."

Brijit smiled uncertainly and reached for it. But as she took it, Raspella's strong fingers closed around her upper arm in a grip like a vice. Brijit looked at her, startled.

The kind emotion was wiped from her instructor's face, and for the first time Brijit saw the true Raspella beneath. It was as if her normally calm face was etched in stone, her eyes filled with hatred and anger. If she didn't have such a strong hold on her, Brijit would have stepped back from the hag that appeared in front of her.

"I would have done the same as you, my dear. I have trained you well. Keep the information you discovered close to your heart and keep yourself safe." Brijit didn't have time to process her shock. Then Raspella emphasized, "It is imperative that you stay safe. You are an integral part of the Prophecy."

And before Brijit could respond, Raspella released her and swept from the room without a single backward glance.

Brijit's legs were shaking and threatened to give out. She sat on the edge of her bed, drawing in some deep breaths, gasping for composure. This is could only mean one thing: Raspella knew she had seen the letter and perhaps she knew that she had taken the map.

Brijit shook her head. Of course she knew. She cursed her own stupidity. Her mentor wouldn't normally have left such an important piece of correspondence just sitting on her desk. Nor would she have been absent for an entire afternoon from her labs and left her office door unlocked. She had done all those things intentionally.

Brijit closed her eyes and shook her head. How could she have been so stupid? Raspella wanted her to find out about the change in plans, but why didn't she just tell her? Brijit smiled bitterly. It was obvious, wasn't it? Raspella would have been forbidden to tell her. She couldn't stop Brijit from snooping around, though. She had always believed Raspella was one of her only allies at the Academy. Perhaps the potions instructor had truly been on her side all along.

But then why did the letter suggest that Raspella had objected to her being selected? What reason could Raspella have for speaking against her?

Unless she knew more about what was in store for her star student than Brijit imagined, and she had been attempting to keep her safe. A shiver of fear ran down her back.

She looked at the small bag that was still in her hand, the one Raspella had been offering her. Opening the drawstrings, she saw that her mentor had put together a kit filled with herbs and remedies Brijit might need on her travels. Another kindness that seemed to go against what Brijit had discovered that afternoon. Raspella's motives were too muddied to see clearly.

Brijit reflected on the events of the evening. She frowned, thinking about how the Elders were so easily swayed by the headmasters of the two institutions. From their demeanor upon entering the ceremony it had appeared that they expected the *Coimirceoirí* to do as they instructed. But they had backed down quickly. It seemed that the headmasters had more sway with the Elders than they would have the students believe.

With a sigh, Brijit returned to her packing. Carefully she tucked the small bag Raspella had given her into her saddlebag. She had a feeling that she was going to be glad that she had that particular gift.

She reached into the side pocket of her saddlebag to make sure the map was still there. But before she could pull it out and study it, the door to the room swung open and Elsa and Serena entered.

"Brijit!" Elsa exclaimed.

Brijit left the map where it was and turned to hug her friends. "I was getting worried about you two. It's so late."

"We were told you were gone," Serena told her.

"What?"

"All the students were told that you and Weylon had left with the Elders."

Brijit shook her head. "Mistress Cowan told the Elders that they couldn't have us until morning because we needed time to pack."

Serena looked at her sharply. "Mistress Cowan argued with the Elders?"

Brijit nodded. “I was surprised, too. But she was adamant that we not leave until dawn. The Elders agreed, readily. They didn’t even question what she was asking.”

“Wow,” breathed Elsa. “I didn’t think any *Coimirceoirí* would challenge an order from the Elders.”

“Neither did I,” Brijit admitted. Then a thought occurred to her. “But perhaps that’s how they want students to interpret the dynamic. If we think *Coimirceoirí* have no power in our relationship with the Elders, then we will be more willing to accept what the Elders ask of us.” She paused and then shifted the topic back to what her friends had said. “Hold it, why were you told we were already gone?”

“That’s a good question,” Serena remarked drily. “Not only were we told you were gone but we were told to sleep in the West Dormitory tonight.”

Clearly the Academy instructors didn’t want her friends to see her. But why?

“We snuck out,” Elsa added unnecessarily. Brijit would expect nothing less from them.

“Of course you did,” she remarked with a grin, then she sobered up. “The question remains, why did they want to keep us apart?”

“I don’t know,” Serena mused, “perhaps it has something to do with what we overheard.”

“Do you think they knew you were there?” Brijit asked in concern, hoping this wasn’t the case. She didn’t want to think that her friends might be in danger.

“I didn’t think so, but now I'm starting to wonder –” Serena trailed off.

Tired of waiting for her friends to explain, Brijit blurted out, “What *did* you discover?”

Elsa flopped on her bed and began to tug her boots off. Serena started to pull pins from her golden hair. “Some of it you already know. Obviously that you’re the Academy apprentice this year and that you’re not going to Sérémela.”

Brijit nodded.

“But they spoke of a Prophecy and a mark and a lot of other stuff we didn’t understand,” Elsa piped in.

Brijit stomach dropped and she thought about the body of the small child in Merryville. Bile rose in the throat. “What did they say about the mark?” she asked.

“Not much. They said, ‘It has begun,” whatever that means, and then Raspella told them that the mark was beginning to appear. It made little sense to us but it definitely meant something to them.”

Brijit frowned.

“Does that mean something to you, Brij?” Serena asked with concern.

Brijit nodded then shook her head. “Maybe…I don’t know.” She looked up at her friends and saw the worry on their faces. She hadn’t told them about what had happened in Merryville. Even though she was angry with Raspella for not discussing it with her, she had still kept her promise not to tell the others. Now she didn’t know why she had kept that confidence.

“I need to tell you something, but promise you won’t get mad at me for keeping it a secret.”

Elsa sat up, her pretty face creased with concern. “What is it?”

“Remember when I went on my last healing test with Raspella few months ago?” Her friends nodded. “Well, something happened that Raspella made me promise to keep to myself. But I think I need to tell you.”

Her friends were silent as Brijit outlined what had happened in the village. When she finished, her friends had identical expressions of horror on their faces.

"The villagers actually killed the child?" Serena asked.

Brijit nodded. "That's what Raspella led me to believe."

"And she said it was a good thing? What kind of person says it's good to kill a small child?" Elsa's voice echoed with the horror Brijit had felt when she first discovered the little girl's body in the town hall.

"She said they were acting on Elders' orders."

"But why?" Serena asked, her voice filled with disgust. "What possible reason could they have for hurting an innocent?"

"The child had a distinctive mark, like a tattoo, on her shoulder," Brijit told them.

"Who would tattoo a child?" Elsa asked, her eyes widening in shock.

Brijit shook her head. "I have no idea. I just know that the reason they killed her seemed to be related to the mark on her shoulder. Raspella insisted that they show it to her before she confirmed that the killing was carried out according to Elders' orders."

"What did it look like?"

Brijit looked at her friends and then closed her eyes. She had to trust someone, and judging by their response to what she'd told them, she felt that she could trust Elsa and Serena. Brijit reached inside her robe and pulled out the pendant Grandmamma had given her. "It looked exactly like this."

Elsa let out a hiss and jumped off her bed, her eyes filled with horror. "Where did you get that, Brijit?" her voice shook.

Brijit looked at Serena, surprised by Elsa's reaction. Serena looked equally confused by the dramatic response.

"My grandmother gave it to me. I thought it was just a family heirloom." She saw the horror growing on Elsa's face. "What do you know about it, Elsa?"

"That's a triquetra, Brijit. It is used by magik wielders. Is your grandmother a *Kurunii*?"

Serena was staring at Brijit with an expression of horror on her face now as well.

"No!" Brijit said, surprised. "Grandmamma is the village wise woman. She is not a witch."

"She doesn't wield magik?" Elsa asked doubtfully.

"No!" Brijit exclaimed again even as doubt began to filter through her. A memory of her grandmother in her herb- and potion-filled kitchen with a pot simmering on the stove surfaced. Not unlike Raspella's potion room, except Grandmamma was known to sometimes chant over her recipes. Brijit hadn't thought anything of it. She assumed all wise women did the same.

She tried to remember what she knew of the *Kurunii*. They were a dying breed. The Elders had outlawed witchcraft in Five Corners. Her grandmother had been very vocally opposed to the law that had come down about a decade ago, insisting that it was discriminatory to women in general and wise women in particular.

Brijit remembered her grandmother's angry words when the law had been imposed. "The Elders have always thought that they are the only ones who have the right to wield magik but they waste it, causing more harm than good. They don't treat it with the respect it deserves," she'd fumed.

Brijit had always assumed that Grandmamma was so outspoken against the Elders because they were privileged in Five Corners and paid little mind to the small villages and poor residents that her grandmother helped. But now she thought about it, she couldn't help wondering if Grandmamma had a more vested interested in protesting the Elders' ban on magikal use outside of Séreméla. What if her grandmother's very livelihood depended on the use of magik?

Brijit looked at her friends in shock. She shook her head even as the pieces came together. How the Elders had started trying to recruit her and take her away from her grandmother as early as her sixth birthday. How her grandmother had steadfastly refused to let her train with the Elders at the Academy until Brijit was old enough to insist that she be given a chance. How absolutely against her leaving Grandmamma had been.

Brijit sat on her bed and stared at the pendant in her hand. Could it be that Grandmamma was of the *Kurunii*? And if so, what did that make her? Was she the granddaughter of a witch?

"Brijit?" Serena said softly. "Are you okay?"

Brijit looked at Elsa. "What do you know about Kurunii in Five Corners?"

Serena spoke before Elsa could, "Brijit, we covered a whole unit on them in third-year history class."

Brijit shook her head. "I didn't. Remember, Raspella had me go on a special training assignment in the Lowlands at that time. I was exempt from the winter term that year."

They stared at each other in shock. Brijit couldn't help wondering what other subjects she had missed the year Raspella sent her away to train.

Elsa licked her lips and seemed to be choosing her words carefully. "Listen, Brij, what we know of the *Kurunii* is only what the Elders and our instructors have told us. In small villages they are revered for their leadership and healing skills. So don't panic. But I do know this," she paused and looked at the pendant in Brijit's hand. "That symbol can only be worn by direct decedents of the Kurunii. All others would be burned by the pewter. It is a magikal talisman, meant to protect."

Serena interrupted, "Is it possible the child could have been burnt by the symbol, like a," she searched for the word, "like a brand?"

But Brijit shook her head. "It didn't look like a brand. It looked like, like a tattoo that the Army members have. But only one and about this small." She held her thumb and index finger together.

"Whatever the symbol is, I think, given the child was killed, we can assume it is the mark we heard them talking about this afternoon."

Brijit's head was spinning, but she forced herself to focus on what Elsa was saying.

"What did they say about it?" she asked.

"They said the mark was beginning to appear, just as the Prophecy predicted. And that measures were being taken to eliminate the problem. But they didn't know if those measures would be enough."

"Did they say why I was being sent to The Rift?"

Serena shook her head. "No. But it was clear that they weren't happy about the decision to send the chosen apprentices there."

Elsa nodded. "They didn't seem very happy with the Elders at all, actually. One might think they were talking on the verge of rebellion. It was pretty strong language they were using."

Brijit was surprised. She knew there were some *Coimirceoirí* instructors who didn't like the amount of control the Elders had over Five Corners, but she hadn't expected the headmaster and mistress of the respective schools to be in that camp along with some of their top instructors. No wonder they were meeting in secret.

"They also talked about the Elders trying to take control of the Alliance, whatever that is," Elsa said.

Serena nodded. "Yes, they said they had to bide their time but that the *Draíodóir* were becoming especially resentful of the Elders and their high-handed ways of doling out magikal licenses outside of Sérémela. They seemed to think that would bring the *Draíodóir* over to their side."

Brijit swallowed hard. If the *Draíodóir* were involved, this could get very ugly, very fast. This ancient sect of druids was the most powerful of the magikal wielders in Five Corners. Each of them was born with an ability to harness magik. They were feared by most of the people in Five Corners, and even the Elders were leery of them. Grandmamma had never had anything good to say about them. And this was the first Brijit had heard of anything called "the Alliance." Alliance with whom?

The knowledge they had before them was very dangerous even if they didn't know exactly what it all meant. If anyone found out that three students knew as much as they did, Brijit had no doubt their lives would be in danger.

"We can't let anyone know about this," she said urgently.

Serena and Elsa nodded.

"Do you think anyone knew you were there?"

The emotion in Serena's turquoise eyes was serious. "I think if anyone knew we were there, we would be dead by now, Brijit." She paused. "But Raspella does know you were aware of the child with the mark, and it appears the Elders, at least, know what your grandmother is."

She left the question unasked, but it hung in the air as if it had been verbalized. If they knew that Brijit was *Kurunii* born, why had they brought her to the Academy, trained her, and allowed her to see what she had seen? Why had she been selected as the Academy apprentice by the Elders, against her instructor's advice? What role did she play in all of this?

Chapter Four

The girls stayed up most of the night, trying to decipher what their combined knowledge might mean. By the wee hours of the morning they were no closer to unraveling it.

Realizing that sleep was now impossible, Brijit turned the conversation to their futures.

"Where are you two going?" she asked, wondering if her friends' assignments would allow them to communicate with one another. It would be nice to know that her friends were only a letter away, especially with the added burden of knowledge the three of them now shared.

Serena's slight smile didn't reach her eyes. "Bermgarten."

Brijit felt a spark of happiness for her friend. Serena had wanted to go there for so long, and now her dream was coming true. Brijit was just sorry that the revelations of the last day and half had stolen some of Serena's excitement in her placement.

Underneath her joy for her friend, she felt a sense of relief. Bermgarten was a major center. It would be easy to get word to Serena if she needed to.

Elsa didn't look as happy. "I'm going North," she said quietly. "To the very foot of Pinefrest Mountains."

Brijit looked at her in surprise. It was unheard of to send an apprentice to such a remote location.

Elsa gave a wry smile. "I know. I have no idea what they are thinking, but I am going into the frozen North with one male *Coimirceoirí*."

Serena nudged her and laughed, "At least you got assigned a handsome one!"

Normally that would have been enough to spark a giggling conversation about the merits of the boy being sent with Elsa, but not today.

Elsa just rolled her eyes and murmured, “True, but still, it’s so remote.”

It was one of the most remote placements Brijit had ever heard of. For Elsa, it would be torture. She thrived on being surrounded by people.

“Okay,” Brijit said, trying to shine some light on the situation. “Both Elsa and I will be remote and unable to communicate with one another. But you will be easy to get a hold of, Serena.”

Her friend nodded.

“How much do you think we should rely on our partner *Coimirceoirí*?” Elsa asked uncertainly, her usually giggling face unsure. “I mean, it’s not like I will have a lot of friends in the Pinefrest Mountains to talk to. It would be nice to know I had at least one person I could trust to talk to about important things.”

Brijit considered what Elsa was asking. It would be dangerous for any of them to share their concerns with others, at least until they were certain they could trust them. Still, she had to admit it would be nice to have an ally they could each rely on, especially since they would be out of contact with one another for so long.

“I think we have to just see what we can learn about our partners and then trust our own instincts,” Brijit said.

Both the other girls nodded, looking relieved.

But Brijit wasn’t sure their *Coimirceoirí* partners could be trusted. The idea of sharing what she knew with the stony-faced Weylon Forborrow was less than appealing.

To be honest, she wasn’t sure what she thought of the male initiate who had been chosen. She hadn’t had any time alone with him and while they had been marched from the convocation hall he had been disinclined to talk. All she knew of him was what her friends had said, which was hardly anything at all, just that he was the most gifted student in half a century.

And that was another thing. The most gifted…they certainly had advertised that fact a lot. But why? She suspected that both the Elders and the instructors had ulterior motives for spreading such news. She had never heard advance praise for chosen apprentices, and this just seemed to be too much. Everywhere she turned there were whispers about what a “gifted” student he had been. But they were so vague – no one even mentioned what it was that made him so special.

From his appearance, Brijit surmised he was a warfare expert. She shook her head in annoyance at the predictability of the Elders. A female apprentice who was an empath and a healer and a male who was a warrior – it was stereotypical in the extreme. But she couldn’t say that she was really surprised. The more she had learned of the Elders over the years, the more old-fashioned and archaic their society seemed to be.

#

Weylon Forborrow looked at the reddening morning sky with a feeling of foreboding that he couldn’t shake. Red skies in the morning never signaled good things.

Soon they would be on their way. He had no idea where they were going, but he would bet his life that it was not to Séreméla. He had stayed up most of the night conversing with Gregor, trying to coax information out of his old instructor and gauge whether or not he knew anything. But the man was unflappable. In the end, desperate for someone to talk to, Weylon had found himself waking Finn in the wee hours, shaking him until he finally opened his eyes a crack, groaning.

“Weylon, I’m sleeping,” Finn protested and pulled the blankets over his head.

"Finn, wake up," Weylon said jerking the blankets off Finn's bed but keeping his voice low. They were in a twelve-bed dormitory and he didn't want them to be overheard by the other students. "We need to talk."

Finn sighed, ran his hands through his hair and then reluctantly sat up.

Weylon gestured to the door and Finn nodded. Once they'd made their way to the common sitting area down the hall from the dorms, Weylon told Finn about his unproductive conversation with his instructor.

"Do you think Gregor was hiding something, or do you think he truly is in the dark about the Elders' intentions?" Finn asked.

Weylon shrugged. With his gifts, he could usually sense when someone was hiding something from him. He hadn't sensed that his instructor was hiding anything, but Gregor was a master at shielding and he was well aware of Weylon's abilities. He didn't put it past the old man to keep secrets.

"I don't know." Weylon frowned. "But I do know one thing: we are not going to Séreméla. There is no way."

Finn raised his eyebrows. "Why do you say that?"

Weylon gave Finn a look. "Three Elder warriors armed to the teeth. Not the usual way they collect their new *Coimirceoirí*."

His friend nodded in agreement. "Well, there is that. In fact, that whole production at the ceremony was a bit over the top, even for Elders. But, Weylon, what do you think their intentions are?"

Weylon looked out the window at the sky that was slowly growing brighter, the red and pink streaks eerie against the blue. "I don't know but the rumors we heard about The Rift could be true."

Concern flickered across Finn's face. "That would put all of Séreméla in jeopardy."

Weylon nodded in agreement. The Rift was largely unheard of in Five Corners. But some of the *Coimirceoirí*, particularly those who were trained as warriors, were privy to more of the Elder secrets than other students.

Séreméla, the Elders' home, was a tropical paradise on the edge of Five Corners. Although he had never been there, Weylon had heard the stories that said moving from anywhere in Five Corners into Séreméla was like stepping into a magikal realm. A bitterness flowed through him. From all he had learned, he had no doubt that the Elders used copious amounts of magik to maintain their paradise while the rest of the land suffered.

Weylon frowned in disgust. The Elders were constantly punishing the rest of Five Corners for using any kind of magik, but they used it in spades for their own comforts. It was unfair and wasteful. Magik could be used to do good, but responsible practitioners always knew there was a price to using the dark power. They did so sparingly. Even the *Draíodóir*, the Druid sect famous for their magikal powers and distrusted by most of the residents of Five Corners, were careful about when and where they used it. But the Elders seemed to see themselves as a society that deserved different rules than the rest of Five Corners. It was unfair and unjust. And it had the potential to hurt all of the land, not just Séreméla.

What most of Five Corners did not know was that on the western side of Séreméla lay a vast wasteland bordering on a black and toxic sea. Known only as The Rift, it was rumored to house monsters of indescribable horror. Some said The Rift was the reason Séreméla had been created – the only way to stop the darkness from advancing had been to create a magikal buffer, which the Elders had done centuries ago under the guidance of their last great queen: Aibhilín.

But the Elders had been without a queen for too long, and some said their hold over Séreméla was weakening while they continued to use copious amounts of magik to maintain their lifestyle. Rumors abounded about the evil that dwelled in The Rift. Most claimed that one day it would break free of the bonds that held it and swallow up the land.

Of course, it was all legend and rumor. Weylon had no real reason to believe it was true. But whispers had continued to come out of the West. And the Elder Council was becoming more and more nervous. He had heard that the Elder ruler, the current Crown Prince, had taken to disappearing for long periods of time, and his consort, pregnant with their first child, was guarded at all times.

Weylon's mouth twisted. The Elders hoped that their princess was carrying the elusive girl-child who would save their kingdom. Or so the Prophecy – another legend that most of Five Corners wasn't privy to – supposedly stated. Weylon had never seen this Prophecy, but he knew there were those in Sérémela who followed the fragments that had been translated religiously, adhering to everything the Prophecy supposedly said and claiming that the future of all of the land would be determined by the words on those scraps of parchment that still existed.

The Elders took the known pieces of the Prophecy as law. But a complete copy of the ancient text had not been found, and much of the writing on the scraps had never been translated. At first this was because it wasn't seen as important to modern-day Sérémela but later, as the Prophecy's following grew, the Elders found they were unable to translate the bits of the document in their possession because it was written in an ancient Elder dialect that was almost completely forgotten today. Only the *Draíodóir* and a few ancient Elder scribes knew anything about the dialect, and none of them were fluent in it.

It was due to their devotion to the mythical writings that the Elders had been waiting for a female ruler for twelve generations. Of course if the first child born to the current royal family was a boy, he would be much loved, but it was understood that he would only be a Crown Prince, like his father. The Elders had been without a queen for many years, and their hopes lay with the child sleeping in the princess's womb. Only a queen could make decisions for the Elders without needing guidance from the Elder Council.

As Weylon understood it, not everyone wished this girl-child would come. There were some who wanted the princess to give birth to a son. Then there would be no official ruler, just another Crown Prince who would be guided by the council. The Elder Council was split between wanting a queen and wanting to continue to make most of the decisions for the people.

It was more than politics behind the Elders' wish for a queen. Weylon did not understand it all, but he sensed the growing desperation in the Elder Council members who had met with Gregor and the other senior *Coimirceoirí*. There had been many closed-door meetings that Weylon could not access, even with his abilities. Those meetings had been carefully shielded, which was suspicious. He had heard snippets of the Prophecy mentioned as well, but when he had pushed Gregor on the topic, his mentor had become angry and silent.

There was so much Weylon did not understand, but he knew enough about politics to know that he and the *Coimirceoirí* female apprentice were stepping into a potentially dangerous situation.

Finn shifted beside him, sensing his dark thoughts. But Weylon kept them to himself. The less his friend knew, the safer he would be.

"Do you know where you will be sent?" Weylon asked, changing the topic abruptly.

Finn nodded slowly. "The Wastelands." His tone was flat.

Weylon looked at his friend closely. Finn looked miserable. "Why would they send you there?"

It didn't make sense. The Wastelands were on the outer reaches of the Outlands. While they were farther south than The Rift, the land there had been touched by the evil, long ago. Nothing grew in that part of Five Corners and as a result, almost no one lived there. It was unheard of for the Elders to send two *Coimirceoirí* there.

"I don't know," his friend answered with a dark expression. Finn was a gifted *Coimirceoirí*, not as talented as Weylon, but, in any other year, he would have been one of the top picks of the class. He just had the misfortune of being Weylon's peer.

"Who are they sending with you?" Weylon couldn't help asking, trying to imagine which of the silly girls would be accompanying his friend.

"No one."

Weylon stared at him in disbelief. "They never send *Coimirceoirí* apprentices on assignments alone."

Finn gave him a bitter smile. "I guess they do now."

Chapter Five

Just before dawn, Brijit had hugged and said goodbye to Serena and Elsa, promising to send messages to Serena in Bermgarten when she could. Elsa promised to do the same. If either of them were moved to less remote locations, they would contact each other through Bermgarten.

On the way to the stables, Brijit had detoured to Raspella's rooms, hoping to have one last word with her instructor and try to get a better feel for where her true loyalties lay. She was surprised to find her mentor's door slightly ajar when she arrived. While she didn't mean to eavesdrop, before she could turn away she heard angry voices that gave her pause.

"They should tell them where they are going," Raspella's voice was shrill.

"The Elders will not divulge that kind of information to students. They haven't even told me exactly what their plans are." Brijit recognized the rough voice of the male *Coimirceoirí* schoolmaster, Gregor.

"Then how do you know…"

"I have ways of intercepting messages, Raspella." Brijit had cringed at the man's superior tone. She waited for Raspella to react, but she stayed surprisingly quiet as Gregor went on. "It is the only way we can stay at all informed of what is happening now. The Elders are becoming more and more secretive." He paused. "But I fear they are sending them to The Rift."

"They *are* sending them to The Rift," Raspella replied with a sneer in her voice.

"How do you know –"

She cut the older man off. “We also have our ways, Gregor. But no mind, what I want to know is *why* they are sending them to The Rift.”

Gregor’s voice was dark as he replied. “I do not know. But I do know their interest in Weylon and his skill set was intense.”

“And Brijit? Why are they so interested in her?”

“You know very well how important she is to them. Her skill set – the empathic ability combined with healing is needed for some reason.” He paused. “And she has more skills than just those.”

Brijit froze. Did everyone know about her supposed *Kurunii* blood? She held her breath and listened hard, not wanting to miss her mentor’s reply.

Raspella answered. “That is not to be spoken of, Gregor. She doesn’t know about it herself. We removed her from her grandmother’s home before she was of age to begin her practice.”

The old man growled. “I told your headmistress over and over that her special skills needed to be developed rather than ignored as the Elders wanted. We are sending her out unprepared. She cannot fight what she already is.”

“You know the Elders were adamant that we keep those skills hidden. I never understood why. But you know what happens when one of our kind disobeys the council.” Raspella paused and then whispered vehemently, “They want one they know will be loyal.”

Gregor grunted in reply.

They were silent for a moment. Brijit held her breath and waited.

“If the queen carries a girl-child,” he said slowly, “she will need a healer who is true and not invested in Elder politics.”

“But The Rift?”

Gregor shook his head. “I don’t know all their motives, Raspella, but I do know this: untranslated fragments of the Prophecy are being pieced together by the Elder archivists. What they discover could change the entire way of life in Séreméla. And you know there will be those who are opposed to that!"

The silence hung heavy in the air again. This time Brijit backed away before she was discovered, her mind racing. She didn't understand half of what she'd overheard, but one thing was clear. The Elders wanted her for more than just her healing abilities. But what that could be, she couldn't fathom.

#

Even with her detour to Raspella's chambers, Brijit was still the first one to arrive at the stables. In spite of her unease regarding what she'd overheard, an unexpected jolt of excitement filled her as she tied her small bags of belongings securely behind her saddle. Regardless of the destination, her time at the Academy had ended.

Her male counterpart, Weylon Forborrow, arrived at the stable before the Elders. If he was surprised to see her there already he gave no indication. Brijit studied him through half-open eyes. He wasn't as tall as she'd thought he was when she'd seen him across the convocation hall; he just carried himself with an air of authority. He was even more attractive close up, but his face was set and closed off. His eyes didn't meet hers, and his only response to her greeting was a noncommittal grunt. Brijit found it hard not to take his silence as rudeness.

She shook her head, turned back to her mount, and stroked the horse's neck. The horse was a beautiful chestnut with dark stockings on his legs and huge brown eyes. Brijit felt her heart melt just a little as he nuzzled her hand and whickered softly. She gave him a quick kiss on his forehead. At least someone on this trip was happy to see her.

"He's a horse, not a pet."

Brijit turned to find Weylon watching her with a sour look on his face.

"He's lovely, and I'm happy to have a mount that's so affectionate. Animals sense how we feel about them, you know."

He looked skeptical but before he could say anything more the Elders arrived. And without further delay they started on their journey.

The sun was just starting to peak over the distant mountains as they headed west. The sky behind them was golden and etched with pink and red. As the sun rose, the road ahead of them lit up in the dawn's soft light. Brijit smiled despite the dark thoughts that had engulfed her over the last few hours. She breathed in the spring air, and a sense of calm flowed over her.

She knew that Séreméla was a two-day journey from the Academy. That's what she had originally based her planning on. For a while now, she had assumed she would be going to Séreméla or, if not there, then one of the other Elder strongholds in Five Corners. All of them were within a day or two of riding. But the revelations from the previous twenty-four hours had changed everything. She tried to gauge what direction they were heading from the slant of the sun as the morning went on. They appeared to be heading directly to the west. She thought back to all she knew about that part of the country. Geography of Five Corners was a required course in second year. But she couldn't remember there being anything about what lay to the west. At the time she hadn't questioned it. As a student with more than enough towns and cities to remember on her final exam, it didn't occur to her to worry about what might be missing. If anything, she had been grateful for less facts to memorize. Now as she reflected on the omission, it seemed odd.

That map she'd found in Raspella's office suggested that a lot lay in the West. Brijit wished she'd had more time to look over that map, but she hadn't wanted to burden Elsa and Serena with it, and she'd had no time since she left her friends to look at it more closely. Now she was with the Elders and Weylon, she didn't dare take it out. It seemed she would just have to bide her time. One way or another, it appeared she would soon find out what really did lie in the West.

Brijit was thankful that she'd ignored the tradition that dictated she wear the Academy apprentice gown on her journey. Instead, she had carefully stowed the ceremonial dress in one of her saddlebags, and instead she had dressed appropriately for a cross-country trip. She wore a long pale green tunic with leather leggings tucked into knee-high boots for comfort while riding. She also wore a warm cloak around her shoulders. She felt confident that she was prepared for this trip. Or at least as prepared as she could be.

But she could have done with friendlier traveling companions. She hadn't expected the Elder warriors to converse with her. Their demeanor at the ceremony had made it clear that they saw the delivery of Weylon and her as a chore. But she had hoped that Weylon would talk to her once they started on their journey so she could get a feel for him. Instead, he steadfastly ignored her, refusing to meet her eye. She knew that she desperately needed an ally, but it didn't look like Weylon Forborrow would fill that role.

As the day wore on, the Elders said very little. Occasionally they would exchange a word or two in the Elder language. Brijit was fluent in their language, but they spoke quickly and in a dialect she didn't recognize. Weylon continued to be silent and stony-faced. Brijit quickly decided that he wasn't worth wasting her time on, and she gave up attempting to talk to him. If he wanted solitude, then he could have solitude. The forest was alive with birds and small animals, and despite her ongoing worries, she felt soothed by her surroundings. She found herself actually beginning to enjoy the journey.

They stopped to make camp only when the sun dipped behind the trees and the path became too dark to see safely. The Elders led them to a small clearing in the woods and then swiftly bade them goodnight. Unfazed, Brijit watched as they disappeared into the trees, without a leaving trace.

Their horses vanished with them. In truth, she was relieved that they wouldn't be with them all night. Although she suspected they might still be watching them from the darkness of the forest.

She turned to look at her fellow *Coimirceoirí*, but he had dismounted and was unsaddling his horse, pointedly ignoring her.

"They won't be making camp with us," he said gruffly, without turning around. Irritation bubbled along Brijit's skin. Did he think she was an uneducated simpleton who wasn't aware of the Elder customs?

Biting back her waspish retort, Brijit slid from her horse's back and gave his neck a firm pat. "I doubt they've gone far," she commented as she began to remove the saddle. Her horse turned to her and nickered softly. She gave him another kiss on the forehead. "You are sweet," she told him softly. Unlike others, she added silently.

Weylon looked over his shoulder in her direction, his eyebrows raised. "Elders don't rest the same way humans do."

Brijit nodded and kept her expression clear, but she was shocked by his word choice. She knew that Elders were different from other citizens of Five Corners, but she was taken aback by what Weylon said. It was almost as if he were suggesting the Elders were not even human. She had never thought of them that way. Elders were surely just a different race of humans living in Five Corners. Weylon's words hinted that they were something else entirely.

Weylon tethered his horse and then looked at her dismissively. "I will gather some wood for a fire. You have food for yourself, I hope."

Anger curled in the pit of her stomach, but Brijit just nodded silently. She was perfectly capable of collecting wood for a fire, but Weylon seemed to think that he was the one who should be doing it. Irritation licked along her nerves as she felt the sexist attitude that the Elders encouraged played out in real life. This was precisely what happened when the boys were educated in a supposedly more rugged environment – they thought they were tougher than the girls. It was ridiculous. She turned back to her horse and began to rub him down for the night. At least she had one friend on this trip.

Half an hour later, she and Weylon sat on opposite sides of the fire. Brijit studied the young man sitting across from her once again, still trying to find some kind of redeeming quality in him. Despite his good looks, his personality appeared to be wholly unappealing. Brijit hoped Serena and Elsa fared better with their *Coimirceoirí* partners, especially Elsa who was going to be so isolated in the North.

Coimirceoirí partners were meant to work as a team. There were many stories about *Coimirceoirí* who had achieved great things by bonding together in their work as guardians of the Elders but there were also countless stories of *Coimirceoirí* failures. Although the inability to bond was rare, when it did happen the consequences were often catastrophic. Brijit hoped Weylon got over his annoyance at having a partner. The sooner he accepted it, the better their lives would be. Brijit wasn't exactly sold on the whole bonding thing herself, but she knew it was inevitable. Eventually they would have to take part in the *Coimirceoirí* bonding ceremony. Not for some time, true, but when it happened she hoped they would be friends rather than enemies.

Weylon was staring moodily into the fire, ignoring her as much as possible. Brijit refrained from rolling her eyes. She didn't have time for moodiness. She was more interested in figuring out where the Elders were taking them and what The Rift was. If Weylon couldn't help her then she would just have to unravel the truth herself.

She'd had a lot of time to think during the ride that day, and while she turned what she'd overheard outside Raspella's room over and over in her head, she still couldn't make sense of it. It was somehow linked to what had been mentioned in the letter she had found in her mentor's desk. But what was this Prophecy Raspella and Gregor had been discussing? It had been mentioned in the letter she'd found as well.

She wondered if Weylon knew any more than she did. He didn't seem surprised when the Elders led them in a direction opposite from Séreméla. Resentment filled her. She didn't put it past the Elders or the Academy to share more information with the male apprentice.

That was another thing: the Elders. For a race that so valued a female leader, they sure had double standards based on gender when it came to the *Coimirceoirí*. The Elders believed that their ruling bloodline would be passed down through the female members of the royal family. Male children were not allowed to rule. Instead they were deemed Crown Princes and the Elder Council guided them in all decisions. Although it had been centuries since their last female ruler, Queen Aibhilín who had sacrificed her own life to safe her people, the Elders still held firmly to the belief that a female ruler would save their people and Five Corners.

It was interesting how the female monarch was treated almost as a god by the Elders, and yet female *Coimirceoirí* were certainly treated as inferior to males. Brijit didn't know enough about the Elder society itself to pass judgment on how they treated their own women. She wondered if women and men were given equal opportunities. The Elder warriors who were leading them on this journey were all male.

Brijit paused as she turned to her saddlebags and began to unpack her sleeping roll. She looked back to where Weylon was sitting and wondered how much he knew about the Elders. What could be the root cause of his coldness? She considered trying to probe his mind to get a feel for what his feelings were underneath that steely exterior but then decided against it. If he were truly as gifted as he was rumored to be then he would sense her invasion immediately and something told her she didn't want that.

His features were still overshadowed by the scowl that seemed to have permanent residence on his face. Brijit decided it wasn't worth attempting yet another conversation. She had tried to be friendly more times than he deserved that day.

He seemed perfectly content to sit in awkward silence. Brijit took a small round of cheese, a dark loaf of spelt bread, and some dried nuts, seeds, and fruit from her bag.

She looked over at where he was sitting, steadfastly ignoring her. She noticed that he hadn't removed any food from his own supply bags.

"Would you like some?" she asked reluctantly, her grandmother's training in good manners too deeply entrenched in her mind for her to ignore him.

He looked over at the food she had spread carefully on her sleeping roll.

"Is that all you have?" he asked, eying her supplies warily.

Brijit's anger threatened to erupt. Did he think she was daft? The food on her blanket was hardly enough to get her to Séreméla and only then if she ate like a bird, which wasn't what she was apt to do. Why did he think she was such a simpleton?

And then a crafty thought occurred to her. What if she pretended to be as stupid as he clearly thought she was? Perhaps she could trick him into revealing what he knew about where they were going. She looked at the supplies again and hid a smile. Perhaps if she played the role he expected from her, she would get more information from him. Remembering how Serena used to widen those amazing eyes of her and blink them at any man she was flirting with, Brijit looked blankly at Weylon, forcing a look of confusion to her face.

"If it is, you'll need to conserve it," he said in the same gruff tone he'd used earlier.

Brijit looked down at the food, forcing herself to act innocent and naive.

"I'm sure I have enough. After all, we'll be in Séreméla by tomorrow evening, don't you think?" she asked sweetly, hoping her expression was as open and trusting as possible.

For the first time his eyes met her own. She just barely refrained from reacting to the contempt she saw there.

"We are not going to Séreméla," he said slowly, carefully enunciating each word, as if he were speaking to someone who was lacking in both intellect and common sense.

Brijit started. Did he know where they were going? She stared at him in feigned shock, her mind going a mile a minute. She wondered what he knew that she did not? She focused on keeping her features clear and shielded herself in case her act wasn't convincing enough and he decided to probe her thoughts.

He studied her for a moment longer and then muttered an oath under his breath. When he said nothing further, she spoke.

"What do you mean we aren't going to Séreméla?" She wanted to cringe when she heard the silly tone of her voice. Instead she focused on looking confused and went on, "Of course, that's where they are taking us. That's where they always take *Coimirceoirí* apprentices."

Weylon looked hard at her. "Seriously?"

Brijit wanted to flinch at the insulting tone he had adopted. Instead she widened her eyes even further and stared at him as if dumbfounded.

"Séreméla is that way." Weylon pointed over his shoulder, north from where they were. "We have been traveling west since we left your Academy."

Southwesterly if he were to be specific. She had noticed the slight shift in direction immediately after their midday meal. But Brijit kept her mouth shut and her features clear of any of the knowledge she possessed.

"I'm sure there's some explanation," she said softly after a few minutes, making her tone just shy of desperate.

"Most likely. However, I don't think the Elders will be sharing their explanation with us."

Brijit looked back at her supplies spread on the blanket, pretending to be considering how long the food would last.

She broke off a small piece of bread and took a tiny nibble of her cheese before putting them back in her bag. Then she allocated herself a handful of the nut mixture. She hoped her growling stomach would be worth the sacrifice to get some information from him. She wasn't used to eating so little.

"Don't starve yourself. I have a feeling you're going to need your strength."

Brijit looked over at Weylon.

"But this is all I have…" she lied softly, easily crossing the line from playacting into outright lying. A shadow of guilt pricked at her conscious, but she ruthlessly pushed it aside.

He shrugged. "We can supplement the food with hunting."

The thought of hunting turned Brijit's stomach. She had no desire to kill the innocent creatures in the woods for food. But Weylon obviously believed that such a practice was not only acceptable but their only way of survival. Hiding her disgust, Brijit decided to pretend that she had no idea how to hunt. It wasn't too difficult of an act – she was actually fairly inept at anything other than fishing. He read the expression she wanted him to see on her face too easily.

"You don't hunt?" he asked incredulously. "What *do* you do?"

"I can gather herbs and tubers. I can cook. There is plenty I can do."

Weylon snorted. "Unbelievable," he muttered. "They send a maid and cook with me instead of a *Coimirceoirí*." He shook his head.

White hot anger flashed through Brijit, but she reined it in and made sure her shielding was in place in case he tried to probe her mind. "I am *Coimirceoirí*," she told Weylon, softly but firmly. "Clearly I have a skill set the Elders value for them to choose me as the Academy apprentice of this year. They would not have done so if they didn't feel they needed me."

Weylon looked into the fire, his expression set.

#

Weylon knew he shouldn't have been so hard on the *Coimirceoirí* girl. It wasn't her fault they were in the predicament they found themselves in. But he was irritated. And there was no one else to take this frustration out on.

The Elders were treating them as little more than servants, and the girl seemed just as dense as the others at the Academy. He shouldn't be surprised, but he had hoped that she would be different.

When he'd first realized that the dark-haired girl from the ceremony was the *Coimirceoirí* who would be accompanying him, he'd felt a flash of hope. She, at least, had seemed to understand that their position was sacred. But after a day of riding with her and their conversation in camp that evening, it appeared that she was no better than the gaggle of girls he'd seen at the Academy.

He had no idea how she had not noticed the direction they were heading: west and directly for The Rift, just as Weylon had suspected.

His gut tightened as he thought of The Rift. He'd never seen, it but the rumors that circulated at Stone Mountain about it were plenty. There was talk of a dead zone where nothing grew leading to a writhing sea of darkness. And for miles before that a dying forest that was filled with creatures tainted by the dark.

What business did the Elders have there with their chosen *Coimirceoirí*? Typically, those who were chosen were assigned to the royal family in Séreméla. Did this mean the rumors were true and the Crown Prince had fled Séreméla?

Of course, Weylon wasn't supposed to know about those rumors. He'd had the luck to intercept a number of Gregor's letters before he left Stone Mountain. Whether or not his mentor had known that his prize student was reading his personal correspondence was a mystery to Weylon, but he didn't really care. At least he had some information to work with.

Weylon watched the girl as she prepared her bed for the night. He couldn't imagine her holding her own in The Rift. What were the Elders thinking taking her with them? A sudden protectiveness rose in his chest. He forcibly pushed it away. He had not bonded with this *Coimirceoirí*, and he didn't intend to. His plan was to work alone. Gregor had scoffed at that plan, but he hoped to convince the Crown Prince to agree that Weylon would better be able to fulfill his duties as *Coimirceoirí* if he wasn't burdened with a female. He wasn't going to let Brijit get under his skin.

His thoughts returned to the mystery of their mission. He couldn't fathom why the Crown Prince would take his pregnant wife to The Rift. He couldn't imagine why he would do such a thing. What could be so horrendous in Séreméla that the Crown Prince would risk his own life and that of a possible heir in The Rift?

There were too many questions in his mind. His gaze drifted back to Brijit. Once again, Weylon wondered exactly what her talents were. It was obvious that she was not a fighter like he was. She was far too meek for that. But her earlier words rang with truth. For some reason the Elders found her valuable. And he knew the Elders would not choose her based on some half-developed skill as a forager or healer.

What kind of gift could she possess in order to be chosen by the Elders as one of their Séreméla *Coimirceoirí*? Whatever it was it would have to be complimentary to his own talents. He was gifted at warfare and reading others. She would be gifted at peace and reading herself. He pondered that for a moment, forgetting that his gaze was still firmly fixed on the pretty girl in front of him. She looked up suddenly as if she felt his eyes on her and flushed a deep scarlet. Weylon didn't look away. He wasn't one to back down, and she should know that.

She looked down quickly and began rearranging her personal belongings in her bag, clearly flustered. He could sense her unease; it transmitted from her in waves.

"You should learn to cloak your feelings," he advised suddenly, knowing there were others who had the same gift as he possessed; ones who were far less ethical in their wielding of that gift.

She looked up, her brow furrowed. "What do you mean?"

"Your emotions radiate from you too easily. Did they not teach you to shield yourself at the Academy?" The irritation in his voice was obvious, but he didn't care.

The girl fidgeted uncomfortably. After a long moment she answered, "Of course they did. I just wasn't…very gifted at shielding."

He couldn't believe it. How could someone who wasn't gifted in shielding be the chosen *Coimirceoirí* of the year? Learning to shield was a more of a skill than a talent. One just had to practice to become proficient. The only reason she would not be at least competent in the skill would be that she didn't practice the exercises they were given. He tried to hide his annoyance. The only reason for not practicing exercises was pure laziness. He studied the girl in front of him. The funny thing was, she didn't look like she was lazy. And she hadn't acted lazy so far on their journey. A lazy girl would not have rubbed down her horse as she had nor would she have been so careful about packing and unpacking her belongings. No, he believed that Brijit Carnesîr was quite the opposite of lazy. So she was either hiding something or there was another reason why she didn't work on her shielding proficiency.

"Is there a reason you don't practice the exercises?" he asked her.

She looked up guiltily then looked down again and whispered, "No." But her words were tinged with untruths. Weylon watch her for a few moments longer, wondering what else she was lying about. He could push her for a true answer. He considered probing her mind but rejected that.

There was no point in using his talents now. Better to wait until the girl trusted him enough to share her skill set with him. He decided to leave it. But suspicion prickled at his senses. It was clear that his fellow *Coimirceoirí* had her own secrets.

As Brijit settled to sleep for the night, Weylon sat up staring into the fire. He still had not discerned what the Elders' purpose was in taking them westward. There had to be some kind of reason. And it had to be linked to the Elder royalty.

Not that he was dying to go to Séreméla anyway. Weylon would like something with a bit more adventure than sitting around the Elders' homeland. But he also liked to plan for unexpected events. If they were to go into battle or even to take a defensive stance against something from The Rift, he would like to know what he would be facing when he got there. But it seemed that the Elders had no intention of telling either him or Brijit. They treated them as if they were merely packages to be delivered. Weylon had not really expected anything more, but it still stung to be treated in such away.

He sat up long into the night, turning things over in his mind. But by the time he laid his head down on his roll he still had no answers about what lay ahead of them.

#

Brijit had climbed into her sleeping roll after Weylon had finished questioning her on her lack of competence with respect to shielding. She was thankful that he didn't try to probe her mind for answers even though it was clear that he didn't really believe what she was saying. If he had tried to probe her thoughts, he would have discovered that she was shielded. Sending out nervous energy had distracted him, but she knew that he wouldn't be content with that for long. He was clearly gifted in reading others and while she was confident in her ability to hold her shield even with the most talented probing, she wasn't sure she could hide the fact that she was shielding herself from him.

She tried to rest. But her thoughts were racing. Now that he'd talked to her a bit more, she wasn't sure playing dumb was the best approach to dealing with Weylon. Still, she was willing to try anything to discover what her fellow *Coimirceoirí* knew about their assignments. And she didn't know if Weylon was a person she could trust – until she was confident that he was not working with the Elders, she wasn't going to let her guard down.

Whether Weylon Forborrow knew more about their destination than she did was unclear. But now she'd ensured that he wasn't going to share his suspicions with her; he thought her incompetent at best and a total airhead at worse.

The last remnants of Brijit's calm trickled away. It was replaced by too many questions to answer. Where were the Elders taking them? What was the Prophecy? What did the mark mean? Were there other children who had been killed? And, above all, what did Weylon Forborrow know about any of it? She fell asleep with those questions ringing in her head.

Chapter Six

The Elders had to know that neither Brijit nor Weylon would have enough food to last them the whole journey. While Brijit had more supplies than Weylon had suspected her of having, she didn't have what she would call an abundance of food, and she wasn't looking forward to foraging for meals their entire trip.

But the Elders seemed to expect that they would need additional supplies. On the third day of their journey, they stopped in a small village.

The settlement was tiny in the extreme, hosting only one inn with a couple of rooms. The Elders seemed to have a prearranged agreement with the innkeeper, an elderly man who had a permanent expression of distrust on his face. Once their horses were put in the stable for the night, Brijit and Weylon were shown to their respective rooms, and the Elders, as per their custom, vanished into the forest.

"Dinner is served in half an hour," the old man told them before he disappeared back down the stairs.

The room Brijit was given was simple but a vast improvement from sleeping on the ground in the forest. It contained a bed and small side table, and that was all. The sheets were worn but clean, and the blanket made of serviceable thick grey wool. There was a chamber pot beneath the bed.

But as Brijit sat down on the edge of the bed, she felt as if she was in paradise rather than a tiny village in the middle of nowhere. Which begged the question, where in Five Corners were they?

Brijit reached into the side pocket of her saddlebag and pulled out the map she'd found in Raspella's office. She studied it for a few moments, trying to decipher the new sections of Five Corners that were outlined and figure out where they were right now, but there didn't appear to be a village on the map that matched the location of this place.

Even though she didn't really have much information on her assignment, Brijit still decided to take the opportunity of being in a village to write to Serena. She knew her friend wouldn't be able to write back since Brijit had no idea where they were going, but she missed both Elsa and Serena and she felt more connected to them by putting her thoughts down in writing.

Dear Serena,

I hope Bermgarten has proven to be all you dreamed it would and that you are getting along well with your Coimirceoirí partner. Weylon Forborrow is just as miserable as we thought he might be. I don't hold much hope of him improving as the journey goes on. I don't know why they called him the most promising apprentice of the last half-century. To me he just seems to excel at grumpiness.

I find myself off the beaten track, which is no surprise. The Elders seem to have their own plans for us, so I don't imagine I will see Séreméla for some time still. I hope Elsa is not hating the remote North too much and I hope you are well. I miss you and will write when I can, although I have no idea when that might be.

Love, Brijit

She finished the letter and put her seal on it and then made for the door, hoping to find the innkeeper before dinner to see if she might be able to get his help in arranging to have it sent it to her friend. Her hand was on the knob when a loud knocking sounded. Brijit pulled the door open to see Weylon Forborrow on the other side.

"Next time check before you open it," he growled at her.

Brijit blinked at him in annoyance. "What?"

Weylon looked like he was going to explode. "Don't ever just open your chamber door without checking who is on the other side, especially in a public house."

Brijit refrained from rolling her eyes. Weylon was being a bit over the top. She hardly thought the old man who ran the inn was going to ravish her. And there weren't any other guests at this point in time. At least none that she'd seen. She rather doubted the inn did a thriving business, given that it was located in the middle of nowhere.

As if he could read her mind, Weylon went on, "*Coimirceoirí* must be careful at all times, Brijit. Readily trusting others can result in harm to both yourself and the Elders you will be assigned to."

As you've clearly illustrated with your lack of trust in me, she thought to herself silently.

Aloud she said, "Okay, I'll be more careful." Her tone was just short of sarcastic, and the words were out before she remembered that she was supposed to mild and meek and naive. Weylon's eyes narrowed at her and then he noticed the letter in her hand.

"What is that?" he asked, grabbing it before she could protest.

"That is a letter to my friend. Give it back. Hey!"

But he ignored her, holding the letter out of her reach before he broke the seal on her correspondence, unfolded it and then scanned the contents.

"That's none of your business!" she protested.

"You can't send this," he told her frankly.

"Why not?" Brijit asked.

"Because we can't give any hint of where we are."

"But I have no idea where we are, and I've not given anything away in the letter, as you can see by the contents."

His eyes dropped to the paper in his hands and he scanned the contents again. He raised his eyebrows and then looked at her, "Excel in grumpiness, do I?"

Brijit felt her cheeks heat. She'd forgotten that she'd written about him.

"Give it back," she said trying to take the letter from his hand.

"No," he said with a laugh and Brijit froze. His entire face changed when he laughed. He looked friendly and handsome and…younger.

"What?" he asked as he noticed her sudden fixation.

Her cheeks burned even more. "Nothing," she mumbled. "I just want my letter back."

He handed it back to her but said, "You really can't send that, Brijit." When she opened her mouth to argue, he held up his hand. "I know you don't mention anything that could lead the reader to know where we are, but how do you think it would be delivered?"

Brijit paused.

"Whatever messenger would be dispensed would be easily traced back to here. And we have to make sure that doesn't happen."

Brijit's spirits sank as she realized he was right. Not that she was about to admit it to him. She stuffed the letter into her pocket and changed the topic, "I'm starving. Aren't you looking forward to a home-cooked meal?"

That seemed to appease him for the moment as he fell into step beside her. Without talking about their plans, they went to the common room together and sat at the same table. Brijit was surprised to find that the common room of the inn was both larger and busier than she'd expected, given how few rooms the innkeeper kept for guests. It appeared that his first business was running a tavern rather than an inn.

Weylon became less irritable as huge bowls of steaming stew and crusty bread were set in front of them, alongside goblets of fresh water.

Conversation wasn't necessary as both of them greedily dug into the first warm meal they'd had since the ceremony at the Academy.

Once she'd scraped her bowl clean, Brijit sat back and looked about the bustling public house. She was surprised to see so many travelers – clearly this tiny settlement was a crossroads for many in Five Corners. She looked up about to mention the fact to Weylon and found him staring at her with a mix of horror and admiration on his face.

"What?" Brijit asked.

He gestured to her now-empty bowl. "I've never seen anyone eat so much so fast."

Brijit flushed again. She had, admittedly, inhaled her food. She'd been eating like a bird on the trip thus far so Weylon would think she hadn't packed as much food as she had. But the warm, well-prepared meal in front of her had been too hard to resist. She felt gloriously full.

"I guess I was hungry," she said softly.

Weylon laughed, and once again Brijit was struck by how his face transformed when he let down his guard.

"The innkeeper told me that tomorrow there will be a public market in the main square. We should be able to buy supplies there."

Brijit nodded, wondering when Weylon had the time to talk to the innkeeper, but before she could question him, the serving girl came by their table with plates of apple crumble for dessert. The girl smiled widely at Weylon as she refilled his goblet of water. But she was wasting her time, Brijit thought, as Weylon paid her no heed – he was good at ignoring flirting girls, it seemed. She couldn't help wondering if he'd had lots of experience doing so.

Brijit devoured the apple crisp, savoring the sweet, tartness of the dish, a smile of bliss on her face. She grinned in Weylon's direction as she found herself relaxing with a full belly and the thought of the warm bed that was waiting for her. She was surprised when Weylon suddenly stood. She looked up at him.

"Let's go for a walk," he said quietly, his eyes darting around the room suspiciously.

Wondering what had put him on edge again, Brijit shrugged and followed him from the great room. She would have preferred to just go up to her rooms and get a good night's sleep, but it appeared that Weylon had other plans.

#

Weylon had noticed a change in Brijit since they arrived at the village. She seemed more confident than she had when they were alone in the forest. Something felt wrong about the whole thing – he couldn't put his finger on it, but she seemed different in some way. Unease filled him as they stepped into the street and walked toward the river in the dimming light.

Refraining from sharing his thoughts with her, Weylon decided to test just how open her mind was to him. He probed for a few minutes, secretly, attempting to enter her mind unawares. Almost immediately he was assaulted with a myriad of emotions. Fear, pride, humiliation, sadness, excitement. The feelings were so overwhelming and so numerous that Weylon had to sit down as a sudden wave of nausea threatened to overcome him. And then just as suddenly he was shut out, the emotions, the thoughts, everything completely silent and black.

He took a few deep breaths, watching Brijit with confusion. She stood in front of him, breathing hard, her eyes flashing with emotion like he'd never seen in her before. She not only knew how to shield expertly; she knew how to open herself more than anyone else he had ever met.

He'd never encountered a mind so open and so busy. There was so much going on behind her seemingly calm exterior that it was impossible to focus on any of her individual thoughts. And she'd been so strong when she'd flung him out. Clearly his fellow *Coimirceoirí* had, as he'd suspected, been keeping some fairly large secrets from him.

Brijit was glaring at him. "How dare you?" she said, rage infusing her words. There was no sign of the meek and timid girl she'd pretended to be.

Weylon held up his hand. "I didn't mean –"

But she cut him off. "Don't lie to me. You certainly did mean to. You can't just probe someone's mind by accident. I guess it didn't turn out the way you expected, did it?"

He stared at the clearly infuriated girl who was standing in the front of him, rage flashing in her eyes.

"Why did you hide this?" he asked.

Brijit shook her head and turned away from him. She remained silent.

"No? Not so eager to talk now? There's plenty going on in your mind. Why did you pretend to be inept?"

Brijit turned back, her face completely devoid of emotion. "I saw no reason to open up to you, Weylon Forborrow. After all, you certainly weren't prepared to open up to me."

Weylon was silent for a moment. She was right about that. He hadn't been at all friendly or open with her. But that was because he thought she was a simpleton whom he was stuck babysitting. He had no idea she hid such talent.

He should have known, he reminded himself. After all, she was this year's Academy apprentice. It wasn't logical that she would be as helpless as she had pretended to be. And he had been so condescending. He shook his head slightly at the memory. He probably deserved this.

She was so strong. He had never encountered a skill set like she had shown. It was something he'd only read of. Suddenly the reason the Elders wanted the girl as one of their *Coimirceoirí* made sense. It was obvious that

Brijit's outer expressions, while they appeared transparent, were only the tip of the iceberg. Beneath the surface raged a multitude of other emotions. And she was able to take one into her mind like no one he'd ever encountered. He had barely probed the surface when he was submerged and threatened to drown. And then she'd flung him out just as easily.

Could she truly be so gifted?

Weylon couldn't help wondering what he would find if reached into her mind again. He turned back to her and saw that she was striding along the riverbank without him. He hurried to catch up. She hadn't gone very far on the isolated path when he overtook her. Reaching out with all his power, he attempted to enter her mind, brutally forcing his way into her inner thoughts. Instantly, white hot pain flash through his skull, knocking him to the ground. He vaguely heard Brijit scolding him from a distance, but he barely noticed her response through the pain that was threatening to rip his head in two.

"What do you think you're doing?"

He finally heard her words through the haze of pain.

"You should learn some manners. Reaching into anyone's mind like that is a violation."

Nausea threatened to overcome Weylon, and his head spun with the emotions that had been unleashed.

He was surprised when she knelt beside him when she saw he was ill. Her anger had faded instantly into concern.

"Here." She helped him lean back against a fallen log on the side of the trail. "Just rest. I didn't mean to push back so hard."

Weylon closed his eyes and waited for the sickness to subside. Brijit sat down beside him, casting worried glances his way now and then.

Obviously there was even more to her gifts that he had suspected. He wondered if she knew just how strong she was? She said she didn't mean to push back so hard, so perhaps she didn't have the training she needed to harness her talents. If so, why would the Elders and her teachers leave such an ability underdeveloped? Surely she could be even more powerful with some training.

#

It took almost twenty minutes for the color to return to Weylon's cheeks. Brijit felt only slightly guilty for pushing him out of her mind so violently. He had no business probing her thoughts, but she could have used a bit of restraint in her reaction to his invasion. Had she pushed any harder, or had he been not as strong, Brijit knew she could have permanently damaged his mind. Guilt pricked at her again, but she pushed it away. He had not been so badly hurt, and he needed to know he couldn't do that to her. Especially since he'd tried to invade her mind not once but twice.

"Are you well enough to go back to the inn?" she finally asked.

He nodded and stood shakily. He shook his head and then began to walk more strongly toward the inn.

They didn't speak to one another, although Brijit could feel the questions he had swirling in the gathering dusk. Instead they entered the inn and went up the stairs to their rooms in utter silence.

As they stepped onto the landing, Weylon let out a curse and began to run toward their rooms.

"Weylon, what are you doing?" Brijit called as she hurried after him wondering what could cause such a reaction. He didn't reply but in a moment he didn't need to, Brijit saw what had sparked his response.

The door to her room was open and two figures were fleeing down the hallway in the opposite direction of the landing. She watched in horror as Weylon chased them only to have them leap through the window at the end of the hall. Brijit caught up to where Weylon was standing at the open window, cursing softly under his breath. Brijit looked down to where he was gazing to see two black figures sprinting across the common and disappearing into the trees.

Weylon turned back to her.

"It seems, Brijit Carnesîr, that you have more than one secret you've been keeping."

Brijit stepped back from the anger she saw in his dark eyes. "What do you mean?"

"Just why would an Elder and a *Draíodóir* be breaking into your rooms?"

Chapter Seven

Brijit stared at Weylon in horror. Her heart hammering in her chest. “Are you sure it was a *Draíodóir*?” she asked, unable to control the shaking in her voice. Fear enveloped her.

Weylon nodded grimly and then gripped her elbow and led her down the hall, back to her room. Her meager belongings had been emptied from her saddlebags and were now scattered around the room.

Tears pricked at Brijit’s eyes. She felt the violation on a physical level. Nausea rolled over her.

“What were they looking for?” Weylon asked as he surveyed the room angrily.

Brijit shook her head as hot tears began to slip down her cheeks. She had no idea why they would do this, and she shuddered as she wondered what would have happened if she had been in her room by herself when they broke in.

Weylon looked at her, obviously impatient for an answer. When he saw her tears his expression changed. He took two steps toward her and pulled her into his arms.

“It’s okay. You’re all right, Brijit.”

Surprise at the physical contact, so gentle and unlike anything she’d ever seen him express, hit Brijit and the tears started to flow in earnest. It wasn’t because the room had been broken into and her things had been looted. It was the culmination of all the betrayal she’d felt in recent months and her deep loneliness. She had been missing Serena and Elsa more than she realized. She even missed Raspella.

Weylon let her cry it out, and when she was finished he stepped away and sat her on the edge of her bed before closing the door to her room. They sat in quiet for a few minutes. Brijit began to feel more and more embarrassed. She shouldn't have lost control like that in front of Weylon. It made her seem weak. But there was no judgment in his eyes when she finally had the courage to meet them.

"Do you know what they could have been looking for?" he asked in a tone so different from his usual gruffness.

Brijit shook her head, the tears threatening again. She needed to get it together. She considered Weylon's question. Why would someone break into her room? She had nothing of value. No money, no jewelry, nothing. "I don't know."

Weylon studied her for a minute and then looked around the room, with an expression of frustration. "Think, Brijit, there must be something you have."

As she looked at her belongings scattered around the room she wondered what they could have been looking for. Suddenly she reached into her pocket and felt the map.

"What is it?" Weylon asked.

Brijit cursed herself for not remembering to shield herself. She closed her eyes. She needed to trust someone, and it seemed as though Weylon was the only person she had right now. She decided to take a chance.

"There is something…" she said softly.

Weylon watched as she pulled the map from her pocket and held it out to him.

"What is this?" he asked as he reached for it and then sucked in his breath as he studied the paper in his hand. "Where did you get this?"

"I took it from my mentor's office before I left the Academy."

He looked at her sharply. "You mean you stole it?"

Brijit smiled sweetly. “If you want to put it bluntly, then, yes.” She watched his face as he continued to look at the map. “Have you seen anything like it before?”

Weylon shook his head. “No. Nothing like this exists at Stone Mountain. At least so far as I’m aware.”

“I hadn’t seen anything like it at the Academy, either. It is very different than the maps we studied in our geography classes.”

Weylon nodded, his mouth set grimily. “It certainly is.”

“Do you think it’s accurate?” she asked.

He licked his lips and looked down, considering. “It is the work of Elder mapmakers, so I would be surprised if it wasn’t accurate.”

“Elder mapmakers – how do you know?” Brijit asked.

He pointed to a small ornate insignia on the bottom left corner of the map that she hadn’t noticed before. “That is the Elder mapmaker’s seal.”

Brijit chewed on her lip and then asked the question that was foremost in her mind. “Do you think that’s what they were looking for?”

Weylon looked around the room and then back at Brijit. “Unless there’s something else you’re hiding, then I think it’s likely.”

Brijit sat down on the edge of her bed and looked at her boots. There was a lot she hadn’t told Weylon, but none of it could be found in her room. She wished she knew whether she could trust him or not. She looked up at him.

He raised his eyebrows, waiting for her to speak.

“I’m sure there are many things that we have both kept to ourselves.” Brijit watched him and saw as his face instantly became shuttered. “I do have things that I haven’t told you. We haven’t exactly been confidants on this trip, but…I’m not sure I can trust you, Weylon.”

“What can I do to convince you that you can trust me?”

Brijit studied his handsome face. In her heart she really did want to trust him but part of her was reluctant.

"Well, perhaps if you shared some of your secrets I would be more willing to share mine."

His mouth twitched and then he nodded. "Fair enough. I know where we are going…"

She nodded, "To The Rift, I know."

Surprised flooded his face.

She smiled grimly. "I found out about that the night before we left the Academy. But what I don't know is what The Rift is, where it is or why we might be going there."

Weylon crossed over to sit beside her on the bed. "I have the answers to the first two parts of your question but not the last."

Brijit leaned forward, eager to hear what he had to say.

"I have never been to The Rift, but I have been told about it."

"By whom?"

Weylon paused and looked down. "It was considered vital knowledge for those of us who were training in combat."

Brijit was silent for a moment, digesting what he'd said. As far as she knew none of the female *Coimirceoirí* had been told about The Rift, whether they trained in combat or not. Or if they had, they'd kept what they were told to themselves.

"Well, what is it?"

Weylon met her eye, his expression serious. "It is a wasteland that borders on a dead sea. It lies on the other side of Séreméla. The Elders' land is protected by an invisible magikal border that is said to have been created during Queen Aibhilín's time."

"Do you have any idea why are we going there?"

Weylon shook his head. "I told you there were some things I don't know. Believe me I tried to get information out of Gregor, but he never admitted to knowing the reasons behind the Elders' plans for us being sent to The Rift."

Brijit considered that for a moment. He knew nothing but he suspected things. She could tell. She knew it had something to do with the royal family.

"I think it might have something to do with the Crown Prince and his heir," she admitted.

"How do you know this?"

"I overheard a conversation between Raspella and your mentor the morning we left the Academy. That was what they said."

Weylon was looking at her with admiration now.

"What?" Brijit asked feeling self-conscious.

"I never took you to be an eavesdropper." Weylon admitted.

Brijit smiled grimly. "I don't think you took me to be half of what I am, Weylon Forborrow," she said suddenly feeling the weight of the talisman that hung beneath her tunic. She wasn't quite ready to share that information with Weylon. In truth, she didn't know if she ever would be.

"I don't think I do," he murmured with admiration, and Brijit was suddenly aware how close they were sitting. She pulled away and stood, her cheeks flaming.

She looked around her room, wanting to lighten the suddenly heavy mood between them. Her few things were scattered everywhere. She bent and picked up her Apprentice gown, folding it carefully, ignoring the muddy boot print that was on the skirt. "Do you think they will come back?" she asked softly.

She heard Weylon rise behind her. "No, I don't think they will but I can sleep on the floor here if it will make you feel better."

Brijit look at the hard floor boards. And then she looked at her bed. Weylon deserved to sleep in his own bed tonight. There was no telling when they would next get a chance to sleep in comfort. She shook her head.

"I will be fine on my own."

He studied her. "Are you sure?"

Brijit nodded. Weylon was in the room next door, she reminded herself.

"Okay. Call if you need anything. I don't sleep deeply." He looked at the map still in his hand. "May I keep this? I'd like to study it a bit."

Brijit nodded. She didn't want to have the map on her body anymore, given that there were those who appeared to be hunting for it.

"Sleep well, Brijit."

"You, too, Weylon."

She watched as he exited her room. Just before he closed the door behind him, he poked his head back in and said, "Make sure you bolt the door tonight."

Swallowing Brijit nodded. He slipped out again, and she knew he was waiting on the other side to hear the bolt slide home. Brijit twisted it and then turned back to the room. She began to gather up her things, folding them and re-stowing them in the saddlebags as she went.

As she worked, she thought about the last few hours. Things had changed quickly between her and Weylon. He now knew far more about her than she had originally wanted. But he had also opened up with her about what he knew of The Rift. She felt that they were easing slowly toward something akin to a partnership. She just didn't know if that was a good thing or a bad thing.

#

Weylon stood outside Brijit's room until he heard her lock slide into place. He didn't think the intruders would try to return tonight. They had come close to being caught – too close, likely, for their own comfort. He was relatively certain they were after the map Brijit had in her possession.

But the question remained, how did they know she had it? It seemed more than likely that her mentor had discovered the missing map and had set the intruders after them. Weylon bit back a growl. That's what he hated most about this business: they didn't know who they could trust.

He returned to his own room and put the map on the small side table beside the bed. He looked at it closely. It was definitely an Elder map, and the only people who knew they were going this way were the Elder knights who accompanied them and those who were close to the Crown Prince.

Weylon studied the map long into the night, committing as much of it as he could to his memory. He stood in front of the dying fire and considered burning it before he made up his mind and shoved it into his jacket. It was dangerous to be carrying the map, but he couldn't be sure he had it completely committed to memory. And besides, Brijit was just starting to open up to him. If he destroyed the map she had let him borrow, he would ruin any chances of finding out what other secrets his *Coimirceoirí* partner was keeping. No, he would hold on to the map for now because if one thing was certain, it was that the girl had more secrets than she had revealed tonight. And after what he'd seen of her gifts, that scared Weylon.

Chapter Eight

As they continued the journey in the days that followed, Weylon and Brijit settled into an uneasy comradery. Now that she had dropped her act of playing dumb, he found she was much as he'd imagined her to be when he'd first noticed her at the Academy. Serious, smart and with a spark of fire that made him like her even more than he thought he would.

He also noticed how the Elders interacted with her, something he hadn't paid attention to before. They treated her with almost a kind of respect. He wasn't sure if she was aware of this attitude, but it was there. They had been told that this one was special; Weylon was sure of it. It should have made him jealous, but it didn't. It just made him feel more protective of her.

Five days after their stop in at the inn, they arrived in another small village. Weylon had been trying to track their journey on Brijit's stolen map, but he had little luck. If he was reading their direction correctly, and he swore he was, then they were heading West. But on the map, there were no villages. There was nothing until Jirgen Forest, the rumored dying woods that were filled with monsters tainted by the dark, and after that Tèarmann. It was as though these villages did not exist, neither on the maps that he had studied at Stone Mountain nor on the Elder-made one.

Weylon felt his anger flare. It shouldn't be surprising that these villages were not on the Elder map. The people who lived in these small, westerly settlements were not important to the Elders. They saw them as nothing, which could be the reason they were not mapped. But they also were strictly rationed on magikal use. They were left to survive as best as they could in an increasing inhospitable environment. The remoteness of their location and proximity to The Rift meant that nothing grew in abundance here. The people who lived in these villages had hard lives. If the Elders had allowed the villages' wise women to use even a small amount of magik, they could have improved their lot. But the Elders were unmoved by their peril.

The irony was that when their oppressors came to town, the villagers were forced to serve them the best of everything. They desperately needed the supplies and cash the travelers brought with them more than they needed their pride.

Weylon knew better than to voice his disgust to the Elder knights they traveled with. In fact, Brijit and he had spoken very little to them. Brijit had become more open with Weylon and more distrustful of the Elders since the attack in the inn. Weylon had convinced her that they should keep that incident to themselves. She had readily agreed.

How far they'd traveled westward was difficult to say. They had left the Academy a month earlier. They were now in a part of Five Corners he'd never explored before. His best guess was that they were below Séreméla's borders. If they turned due north, he was fairly certain they would pass into that land. But they did not turn north, and there was no indication that they would change their westerly course any time soon.

Just as Brijit and Weylon had not known the name of the last village they were in, they were ignorant of this village's name. There were no placards or signs indicating the name of the place, and the Elders they were traveling with certainly didn't play tour guide. Weylon wondered if it had a name at all. He wasn't precisely sure what to expect, but as they rode into the town, he was surprised by what he saw.

The village was tiny, not even big enough to be called a town. The villagers were amongst the poorest he'd ever seen. Their clothing was ragged and their cheeks were hollow and hungry. They flocked to their doors to watch them arrive, curious but not seeming too surprised to see Elders in their village. That was strange. What could a little settlement like this offer to the Elders on a regular basis?

Beriadan stopped outside a rundown house, barely more than a shack. He went inside, leaving them where they were on the street. Weylon looked at Brijit, who exchanged a puzzled glance with him. When the Elder returned, he nodded at his companion who then gestured for Brijit to accompany them inside. Weylon started to dismount.

"Just her," Beriadan told him.

Weylon straightened and looked at them, his senses suddenly on high alert. What did they want Brijit for?

Brijit froze in her saddle. "Why?" she asked suspiciously.

"He is not needed. He can stay out here."

Weylon settled back into his saddle, unease threading through him. He saw how white-knuckled Brijit's hands were on her reins.

She did not dismount. "I would prefer that he accompany me."

Weylon looked at her in surprise. She met his gaze steadily. And she opened her feelings to him, clearly radiating trust toward him…and uncertainty toward the Elders. He flexed his shoulders and made a decision. He was not going to let Brijit go into that dwelling without him.

The tall Elder stepped closer and grasped the bridle of Brijit's horse. He shook his head. "That is not necessary."

Brijit straightened in her saddle and looked down at him. "It is necessary if you want me to go into that dwelling. I will not enter it without my fellow *Coimirceoirí.*"

Weylon was surprised by her firm tone; it went against the fear and uncertainty he knew she was feeling. She was doing a good job of cloaking her real emotions from the Elders. Weylon stared at her in awe – he had never known anyone who could open herself to one person while still shielding her feelings from others.

If the Elders were surprised by Brijit's refusal to go with them, they didn't show it. But, then again, they rarely displayed any kind of emotion, and they were always shielded. It was impossible to probe the mind of an Elder. Beriadan just inclined his head and the tall Elder stepped away from Brijit's mount.

Brijit turned and looked at Weylon once again. He nodded and dismounted. Only when his feet were on the ground did she slip from her saddle to stand next to him. He looked over at her, but she was now focused on the home in front of them. Straightening her spine, she stepped up to the wooden door. He felt her fear for one moment longer and then she shielded herself completely

The Elders watched them with narrowed eyes but didn't try to stop Weylon from following Brijit into the house.

#

Brijit took a deep breath before pushing the door to the cottage open. She couldn't help the feeling of foreboding that was sweeping over her. Something was not right in this place. Even Weylon's presence behind her did little to calm her nerves.

The inside of the cottage was dark and dank, and there was the musty odor of dust and disuse. If Brijit hadn't been brought inside by the Elders she would have assumed the place had been deserted years ago.

Beriadan stepped around her once she was in the small entrance to the house.

"Bellasiel, we are here," he called into the darkness.

To Brijit's surprise, a female Elder came down the stairs and spoke to him in a dialect of their language that she didn't recognize. The woman had hair so pale it was almost white although her face didn't bear a single wrinkle or line. She turned to Brijit.

"Come, *Coimirceoirí*. You are needed."

Brijit looked back at Weylon. He shook his head slightly. His expression was just as mystified as her own. Brijit's heart kicked into high gear as she began to follow the woman up the stairs. Suddenly she felt Weylon's hand on her shoulder in a surprisingly reassuring gesture. Unexpectedly a sense of calm swept through her.

The stairs creaked under their weight, but Brijit was focused on the noises that were coming from the upper floor. A woman was sobbing and gasping. Someone was in pain. Brijit began to step faster.

Bellasiel led her into a bed chamber that had obviously not been used for a long time. There was a thick layer of dust on all the dark, heavy furniture in the room. But she soon forgot the neglected state of the room as her attention was claimed by the young woman who was moaning on the bed.

As Brijit stepped closer, she realized the woman was younger than she had first thought. In fact, she was around her own age, perhaps eighteen. Her dark hair was plastered to her head by sweat and she was clearly in the latter stages of labor. And she was struggling.

"How long has she been like this?" Brijit demanded, but Bellasiel ignored her. How and why this poor girl had come into the hands of the Elders was a mystery to Brijit. But there were more immediate worries at hand. She had started helping her grandmother bring children into the world from the time she could walk, and she was good at it. She had helped birth more than twenty babies before her tenth birthday and had been recognized as a midwife in her village from that time until she'd left to go to the Academy three years later. And all her experience told her that the girl in front of her was in danger.

"I need hot water and some clean towels. Can you manage that?" Brijit asked the Elders who were standing to one side of the room looking at the girl with distrust.

“Can you manage that?” Brijit repeated, but it was Weylon who answered.

“I will see what I can find.”

Brijit was flabbergasted as to why the Elders were just watching the girl suffer. There was no need for her to be in such pain. Shaking her head, she turned to her.

“Try to calm down,” she said softly reaching out and touching her sweat-soaked head. “I can help you but fighting this will only tire you out.”

“They want to take it,” the girl panted. “Don’t let them take my baby.”

Brijit looked over to where Bellasiel and Beriadan were standing impassively. “Can you leave the room? You are only agitating her.”

When they both stood as if she had not said a word, anger flared through Brijit.

“Leave the room now or you risk the death of both mother and child.”

That finally got their attention.

“We will be right outside the room,” Beriadan told her gruffly.

Brijit nodded and turned back to the sobbing girl.

“What is your name?” she asked softly.

“Ana,” she whispered. “Why is this happening?”

“Babies tend to come when they are ready, my dear. Try to calm down, you are not helping yourself or your little one.”

“No, no, no, you don’t understand.” Ana’s eyes rolled in her head and she began sobbing again. “They will take him. They will take him. It’s to punish me.”

Weylon came into the room with some hot water and surprisingly clean cloths.

“What else do you need?” he asked.

"In my saddle bags you will find a small bag that holds a collection of medicines. Can you bring it to me? I want to give her something to help ease her pain."

He nodded and disappeared again. Brijit washed her hands and began examining the girl as best she could, but Ana was writhing so much on the bed that it was a challenge.

"Ana. Please, calm yourself. Your baby is going to come. There is nothing we can do to stop it."

Brijit did not want to ask Ana why she thought the Elders would want to punish her. She wanted to stop her child from being born. The terror that was emanating from her was obvious. It clearly had something to do with the Elders, but Brijit couldn't fathom what that might be. Taking a deep breath, Brijit reached out and placed her hands on Ana's head. She focused on opening and was at once assaulted with so many emotions she almost lost her footing.

Refocusing, she let Ana's emotions pour through her, as she had been taught. Ana was terrified of the Elders. Brijit already knew that, but she could not "ask" the emotions why – she could only open to emotion not to facts. But suddenly she had a strong vision of the triquetra on a chain around Ana's neck. Brijit reached under Ana's shift and felt the familiar pewter she wore around her own neck. Ana was *Kurunii.*

Ana began thrashing, trying to push her hand aside.

"Calm down," Brijit said softly, and she reached into her own tunic and pulled out her grandmother's pendant.

Ana's eyes widened, and she met Brijit's gaze.

"Ana, I won't let them hurt you."

"You can't stop them. That's all they do is hurt and take. Look at our village. They have ravaged it. Look at me." She sobbed. "And now they will take the only thing that is mine."

Brijit was shocked. "Ana, what do you mean? I don't understand."

"They think it is theirs. But it is mine. Mine. I won't let them have him."

"Ana, calm yourself. No one is going to hurt your baby. You need to calm down and focus on breathing."

Weylon returned with her medicine bag in his hand. Brijit was reaching for it when Ana started screaming.

"What is happening?" Weylon asked.

"I don't…" Brijit's eyes widened in horror as she saw the blood beginning to pool beneath Ana. She was hemorrhaging.

"Ana?" Brijit asked as she prepared to catch the baby.

Ana moaned at them, "Don't let them have him." And then her eyes rolled back in her head and she lost consciousness.

The baby landed in Brijit's hands. He was a large babe, with a shock of blond hair and distinctively Elder eyes. An Elder/*Kurunii* child. Brijit look up to where Ana lay unconscious. There was too much blood pooling beneath her.

Handing the baby to Weylon, Brijit moved to Ana's side but the girl was deathly white and not breathing. She felt for a pulse but there was none. Ana was dead.

"Brijit?" She looked over to where Weylon was awkwardly holding the strangely silent child.

"She's dead," she whispered. "Give me the child."

Cradling the small boy, she stepped across the room to where the warm water and towels were placed. She began to clean the baby off, surprised by the way he was studying her. A newborn rarely responded to birthing in this way. Gently Brijit ran the rag over him, cleaning the mucus and blood from his pale skin. She turned him to clean his back and gasped.

"What is it?" Weylon asked.

Brijit stared at the abnormality on the child's shoulder. A black mark exactly like the one she had seen on the dead child in Merryville was outlined on his pale skin. She studied it up close. It wasn't like a birth mark – she had seen plenty of those, including the well-known wine marks that children were sometimes born with. But this was different. A perfectly circular mark with a triquetra within it. It had the appearance of a tattoo but that was impossible – the child had just been born.

Brijit lifted the child gently so Weylon could see his back. "What is it?" he asked as he stepped closer and traced the mark with his index finger. "A triquetra? But that's the mark for…" Weylon trailed off as horror filled his dark eyes.

"The *Kurunii*, I know."

Weylon backed away from the child, shaking his head. "What kind of dark magik is this?"

"I don't know," Brijit whispered, making the decision to not share the fact that Ana was *Kurunii* or that Brijit likely was as well. She didn't want that look of disgust and horror on Weylon's face directed at her. She wondered what about the *Kurunii* so repulsed him?

Weylon's met her gaze, his dark eyes full of questions. "Have you seen this before?"

Brijit nodded but before she could speak, the baby's howls filled the air. Before she could swaddle the child Bellasiel burst into the room. She crossed to where Brijit and Weylon were without a second glance at Ana. It was as if she expected the girl to be dead. Bellasiel moved to take the child. *Don't let them take him*, Ana's words filled Brijit's mind and she instinctively stepped away.

"What are you doing, *Coimirceoirí*?"

Brijit met Weylon's eyes, silently imploring him to help, and he stepped to block the Elder's progress. Bellasiel called out in her language and the door burst open to reveal the warriors who had accompanied them. The threat was obvious.

"Give me the child, Brijit."

Realizing the futility of fighting to keep the boy, Brijit reluctantly handed him over. The female Elder turned him, as if expecting to see the Mark on the child's shoulder. She let out an Elder curse, and before either Brijit or Weylon could react had removed a golden dagger from her belt.

"No!" Brijit screamed but was helpless to do more than watch as Bellasiel quickly and savagely cut the newborn's throat.

Weylon grabbed Brijit before she could launch herself at the Elder.

"Go," Bellasiel said gutturally.

A sob rose from Brijit's throat as she saw the baby's blood mingled with his mother's on the floor. Suddenly she felt very, very weak. Weylon's arm around her tightened and he led her to the door.

Before they stepped through it, Bellasiel said, "And, *Coimirceoirí*," her voice was hoarse with emotion, "forget what you have seen here."

#

Brijit stood by her horse looking up at the house where Ana and her child had died. The Elder knights had not seemed perturbed by the deaths. They were used to seeing horrors in the battles they had fought. To Brijit, however, the nightmarish scene played over and over in her mind.

She kept wondering what she could have done differently, but every time she went over the events leading up to the horrific end, she was at a loss to think of anything she could have changed. It was as if the mother and her babe were doomed from the beginning.

But if that was true then why did the Elders even bother to bring her into the birthing room. If their intention was to kill both of them, why did they need Brijit to try to deliver the child?

Before she could analyze it in full, the Elder knights were telling Brijit and Weylon to mount their horses.

"What was the purpose in this?" Weylon demanded but the Elder knights ignored him. Bellasiel, who had been inside the decrepit shack when they arrived, seemed to have disappeared as quickly as she had come.

As they prepared to leave, Brijit felt another wave of sadness wash over her. She had barely made it out the front door of the cottage under Weylon's support before she had been violently ill in the bushes. She had helped birth many children in her life, but she had never seen anything as tragic as what had happened that morning. Brijit had seen mothers die in childbirth, but she had never seen anyone want to harm a newborn, never mind savagely kill one as Bellasiel had.

Ana had been far too young to die but what she had suggested to Brijit in that upstairs room was far more troubling than even her death or that of her child. That the Elders were somehow to blame for Ana's death. Had they known the girl was *Kurunii*? Brijit assumed they had.

What had happened after Ana's death, what Brijit had seen on the body of the baby, was even more troubling. She closed her eyes but tears pooled beneath her lids and spilled down her cheeks.

"Brijit." She looked up blindly to where Weylon was by her side.

"Shield yourself for now and just ride," he said softly but with a warning edge in his voice. She met his dark brown eyes and understanding dawned. He wanted her to hide her emotional response from the Elders. It was dangerous for her to be too distraught. *Coimirceoirí* were to act on Elder's orders without question. Taking a deep breath, she nodded slightly and then turned her mount to follow him.

They traveled for hours away from the village where Ana had died. The ride was silent. Brijit returned to her earlier musings. If the Elders wanted the child and mother dead, why would they risk the *Coimirceoirí* seeing them. What was going on?

She straightened in her saddle as she realized with a jolt that the Elders must not have known if they wanted the child dead. It was obvious that they cared nothing for the mother. Poor Ana had been left to suffer for what had to have been hours before Brijit was brought to her. By then it was too late for Brijit to do anything more than catch the child. If the Elders had cared about Ana's wellbeing at all, they would have made sure she was comfortable.

It was the infant they were concerned about. Brijit was sure of it. She wondered who the child's father was. Brijit had no doubt the child's father was an Elder. Which Elder she would never know. The knights had hurried Weylon and her from the village before they could ask any questions.

It was that mark on the child's shoulder that seemed to have determined his death. As soon as Bellasiel saw it, she killed the child. Brijit wasn't so sure that he would have been killed if that mark had been missing. But Ana had been sure the Elders would take her child. Once again, Brijit wondered what it could mean. She remembered the conversation her friends had overheard about the Prophecy and a mark and the beginning of something.

Looking at the road ahead of her, she wished more than anything that she could see Serena and Elsa and talk over what had happened in that village with her friends. Together the three of them might be able to piece the puzzle today. But Brijit was alone with only a sliver of the truth. She had to try to figure this out on her own, and she didn't think she was capable of doing so.

Despair washed over her in waves. Delivering a baby was always an emotional experience, but delivering one and losing not just the child but the mother as well was devastating. Brijit knew she couldn't afford to think about it now. Every time her mind threatened to drift back to what had happened, she redirected her attention to the road in front of them.

Her eyes landed on Weylon's broad back. She hadn't told him too much about what she knew of the Elders. She hadn't shared with him all she learned in Raspella's rooms or everything she had overheard the morning before they left. And she certainly had not shared with him what her friends had discovered from their hiding place in the wardrobe. She looked at those shoulders for a while, considering.

She knew that Weylon was trying to piece together what had happened to Ana and her child as well. She also knew that he seemed to sense that she had seen the mark before. She fully expected that he would question her once they arrived at camp and the Elders left them.

Maybe it was time for Brijit to start trusting him.

#

It was late afternoon when they finally stopped for the night. As per usual, the Elders left her and Weylon alone in their encampment without a word. Weylon dismounted and set about preparing the camp for the night, tethering their mounts and making a fire. Brijit sat on a small tree stump near the fire pit Weylon constructed. He let her be, not intruding on her thoughts. But she was grateful when he dropped a blanket around her shivering shoulders. Thoughts of what she had witnessed filled her mind. She couldn't stop wondering what the Elders' purposes were.

They had clearly wanted her assistance in the birthing process but had brought her to the house too late. And once Ana and her child were dead, they wanted her gone as quickly as possible. Why did they need her there in the first place?

If the child had not had that mark, what would have become of him? She remembered Ana's frenzied words. She knew the child was in danger. The Elders had savagely killed the infant, just as the villagers in Merryville had killed that little girl, seemingly on Elders' orders. Why did the Elders want those children dead? Was it because the boy was clearly part Elder? That didn't make sense. The child in Merryville did not seem to have any Elder blood in her. And while it was rare for Elders to mate with village girls, it wasn't unheard of. The baby today wasn't the first child to be born a halfling. It had to be the mark. That was the only thing that tied those two children together.

Brijit shook her head as she stared into the flames of the fire Weylon had built. She was barely aware of him coming and sitting next to her.

"Are you all right?" he asked after a few moments.

Brijit nodded even as tears, sparked by Weylon's gentle tone, pricked her eyes.

To her surprise, Weylon reached out and rubbed her back softly but said nothing more. It was as if their relationship had shifted in that dark room. They had now truly bonded as *Coimirceoirí*. She thought she might begin to tell him some of what she knew.

If she told him what she had found in Raspella's room, what her friends had overheard and the details of Raspella's and Gregor's conversation, then maybe he could help her untangle this mystery. But something told her not to tell him what lay around her neck. She had seen his face when he realized that Ana was a *Kurunii.*

They were both silent for a few moments, staring into the fire. "Weylon," Brijit said softly. She felt him turn and study her face. She stared straight ahead at the fire for several minutes until she was sure she could speak without dissolving into tears.

"I'm scared," she admitted and then looked up at him.

His handsome face held a thoughtful expression. He nodded in understanding. "I think you're wise to be wary," he said carefully. Then he paused and looked at the fire again.

Tired of playing games, Brijit straightened and pulled away from him. When he looked at her she asked, "What do you know about our assignment?"

Weylon's eyes narrowed and then understanding dawned on his features. "What do you know?"

Brijit held his gaze, her mind made up. It was time to have someone on her side. "Not much, but I think we'd better start working together. For our own sakes."

Chapter Nine

Several weeks after Brijit had decided to start trusting Weylon, she was chopping vegetables and adding them to the venison stew when he came and sat across from her, watching her work. She could tell he wanted to talk about something. In the past weeks they had become much more relaxed with one another, and Brijit was starting to understand the *Coimirceoirí* who sat across from her now. She waited patiently for him to speak his mind.

"Have you noticed the woods are changing?" he asked her as he looked around at the trees hugging the clearing they were in.

Brijit paused in her work and looked around. She had, in fact, noticed a marked change in the forest in the last two days. There were fewer and fewer woodland creatures and more and more trees that were dropping their leaves far too early in the season.

She nodded at Weylon. "I have. Do you know why?"

Weylon spread out the map on his knee and studied it for a moment. "I think we are getting closer to Jirgen Forest."

Brijit looked at him questioningly. She had never heard of Jirgen Forest before she had seen the name printed on the Elder map. To her it meant nothing.

"Jirgen Forest is rumored to be a dying wood," Weylon explained. "I don't think we can be fully within its borders yet, but we are getting close. Legend has it that nothing grows in Jirgen, the animals have long since fled and the trees are standing skeletons."

Brijit shivered as she imagined a forest full of dead trees.

"What caused an entire forest to die?" she wondered aloud as she went back to stirring the stew.

"The Rift," Weylon said with certainty. When he saw the confusion on her face, he continued, "I've heard that The Rift's poison is spreading. Séreméla has protected Five Corners for centuries but its magikal borders are weakening, and the evil energy that makes up The Rift is slowly ebbing into the land, killing everything it touches. Jirgen Forest is the closest thing to The Rift besides..." he paused and studied the map again, "besides this forgotten Elder fortress, Tèarmann."

Brijit looked at the letters etched on the map where Weylon was pointing. Tèarmann.

"That is if it still exists," he added drily.

"And you think that's where we are heading?"

Weylon nodded thoughtfully. "I don't see where else we could be. If this map is at all accurate, and as an Elder map I have to assume it is, then there is no other place between here and the Dead Sea."

"But the villages we've just passed through weren't on the map either. How can you be so sure that's where we are?"

Weylon shoved his hands into his hair, frustration on his face. He looked down at the map again. "I guess I'm just going with my gut, Brijit. I think we are going to Tèarmann, but we will have a better idea if we start to pass through Jirgen Forest. That forest is unlike any other in Five Corners."

Brijit shivered and Weylon noticed. He smiled at her, "Don't worry. I have a feeling our Elder guard would not risk either of our lives. For some reason, we are important to them."

Brijit nodded in agreement. She didn't know why but the Elders seemed to value their lives.

"But, Brijit, maybe we should burn the map," Weylon said slowly.

She looked at him in surprise. Burning the map would mean that they couldn't refer to it anymore. Then again, she was sure that Weylon had it memorized by now. He had studied it every chance he had.

"Something tells me that having that map could be dangerous to our wellbeing."

Brijit frowned as she stirred the stew again, "But no one has tried to take it since that day in the inn."

Weylon nodded, "I know. But I still think we would be better to not have it with us. I already know everything that's on it."

Brijit bit her lip considering. In the end, she couldn't come up with a reason for holding onto the map. She nodded, "Okay, we'll do what you think is best."

Weylon gave her a grim smile, looked down at the map one more time and then fed it into the fire beneath their stew pot. Brijit held her breath as she watched it, half expecting some Elder magik to escape the parchment while it burned, but it just shriveled up and burst into flames like any other piece of paper.

"Hey, enough dark talk for the night, let's talk about something lighter," Weylon said after the map had dissolved into black ash.

"Like what?" Brijit asked.

He cocked his head as if thinking deeply. "Like why you decided to become *Coimirceoirí*?"

Brijit frowned as she remembered her grandmother's disappointment in her choice.

"Uh-oh, an unhappy topic," he said as soon as he saw her downcast expression. "Okay, let me go first. Ask me anything."

Brijit smiled at him, a bit disconcerted that he could read her emotions so well when she wasn't shielded. Pushing her unease aside she asked, "Well, why did you decide to become *Coimirceoirí*, Weylon Forborrow?"

"That," he grinned, "is a great story. My older brother was a hero! And all I ever wanted to do was to follow in his footsteps."

Brijit smiled. As a child with no siblings, she loved hearing stories about families. "He was *Coimirceoiri*?"

Weylon nodded. "Not a chosen one but he still led a very adventurous life, at least it seemed exciting to his little brothers."

"How many of you are there?" Brijit asked, smiling as she thought of Weylon as a small boy.

Weylon's face clouded a bit but then he went on with his story. "There were three of us."

Brijit didn't miss the fact that he used past tense, but she pressed her lips together and waited for him to continue with his story.

"Archer, my older brother, was ten years older than me. Fourteen years older than Ren, my younger brother. And Ren and I hero-worshipped him. Our father had died of an illness when we were very small, so Archer took on a father-like quality for Ren and I." Weylon smiled at the memory. "Except Archer was much cooler than any father I ever knew."

"What happened to him?" Brijit asked, intrigued.

Weylon's face clouded again, and she was sorry she asked. But he shook his head and looked at her. "He was assigned to Sailsburg. The Elder he worked with traded with the men of Nasseet."

Brijit sucked in a breath. The Island of Nasseet was not technically part of Five Corners, lying to the south in the middle of the Sea of Arcadia. Their people were known to keep to themselves except when trading in Sailsburg.

"Ah, I see you've heard of our neighbours to the south. Well, my brother had the misfortune of working for an Elder who angered the traders. To be honest, I think the Elders probably tried to skip payment."

Brijit gaped in horror. No one ever tried to rip off the Nasseet traders. It just wasn't done.

Weylon nodded. "They sent Hunters after them."

"No!" Hunters were special Nasseet assassins who had the ability to teleport. No one ever escaped Hunters and lived to tell about it.

Weylon's face was grim. "The Elders that Archer worked for thought they could get back to the safety of Séreméla before Hunters caught up to them. And they almost did. But Revuover wasn't far enough. Everyone in their party was killed in their sleep just outside the gates of Séreméla." Weylon swallowed hard. "Archer included."

"Oh, Weylon, I'm so sorry," Brijit breathed, her heart aching for the little boy who lost the only father figure he had ever known.

He smiled sadly. "It's okay. Archer died doing what he loved. He lived to be *Coimirceoirí*. And his fire and passion for the job only made Ren and I want to join even more."

"He would have been proud of you," Brijit noted.

Weylon smiled at her. "I think he would have," he agreed.

"Is Ren training at Stone Mountain as well?" Brijit asked after a moment of silence.

Now Weylon's face darkened with pain. "Ren is dead."

Brijit's mouth fell open. "How?"

"My younger brother was the biggest risk taker of all the Forborrow boys. He died while trying to cross the river in spring by my home in the Outlands. The raging waters swept him away." Weylon's eyes shone with tears. "They found his body two weeks later. My mother never recovered. She died of heartache a few months later. I guess I wasn't enough for her to live for now she'd lost everyone else."

"Oh, Weylon, I'm so sorry." Brijit's heart ached for him.

His face cleared after a few moments. "But what about you Brijit Carnesîr? What made you want to become a *Coimirceoirí*?"

"I'm not sure that's a happier story," she murmured as she scooped the stew up into their wooden bowls and handed one to him. "I always wanted to be *Coimirceoirí*, ever since the Elders first started to recruit me when I was six."

Weylon paused with his spoon halfway to his mouth, his eyes wide. "Six?! Wow, that's an honour. Your parents must have been very proud."

Brijit looked down at the bowl of steaming food in her lap. "My parents died when I was an infant."

"Oh, I'm sorry, I didn't know."

Brijit shook her head. "It's okay. I didn't ever really know them. My maternal grandmother raised me."

He smiled, "Well at least you were with family. Was she pleased by the *Coimirceoirí* attention?"

"No," Brijit admitted bluntly. "My grandmother hated the *Coimirceoirí* and she never approved of my decision to train with them." She bit her lip. "We haven't spoken since I left her home five years ago."

Weylon looked sorry for her. Brijit tried for a smile and failed. The mood had gone from light and joking to very heavy in just a matter of minutes.

"Well, I guess I chose the wrong topic for tonight," Weylon admitted wryly as he scooped up the last of his stew. "Next time *you* chose the subject."

Brijit laughed at this. "Well, since you chose such a depressing topic, I think it's only fair that you should be stuck doing the cleanup."

Weylon groaned and then got to his feet and collected the dishes without arguing. Brijit found herself smiling in spite of the discouraging conversation.

Later, when she settled in her bed for the evening, that smile was still on her mouth. The conversation over dinner, while a bit dark, had brought her and Weylon closer together. They had more in common than she had originally believed and the thought lightened a weight that had settled on her heart. She had the feeling that Weylon Forborrow and her were on their way to becoming something like friends.

#

The village where Ana had died with her baby was the last "civilized" place they had seen. They moved deeper and deeper into the wilderness of the western realm. Weylon was glad he had burned the map when he did. He sensed that the Elder knights remained close to them now and, after Brijit had insisted on his help with the birthing of that halfling child, he had noticed on more than one occasion Beriadan watching the two of them with distrust in his eyes.

The first night after the child had died, Brijit told him what she had discovered at the Academy. He was surprised that she had been suspicious of her instructors for months before she'd left. He'd had his doubts about Gregor and had pushed him but hadn't doubted his mentor in the same way Brijit had hers.

When Brijit shared what had happened at Merryville, Weylon understood. The fact that the townsfolk had killed that child the same way Bellasiel had killed the infant in the nameless village, and had done so supposedly under Elders' orders, put a chill in his heart. But the fact that Brijit's mentor had refused to discuss what had happened with her, and had forbidden Brijit to tell anyone what she had seen, was even more troubling. Clearly the Elders did not want *Coimirceoirí* apprentices knowing about the mark or the Prophecy. Or hadn't wanted them to. That seemed to have changed now. Neither the knights nor Bellasiel had seemed concerned that Brijit and Weylon had witnessed the killing of the marked child. They had just wanted to make sure neither of them told others about the incident.

Weylon had never heard that any *Coimirceoirí* were mentioned in the Prophecy before. He wondered if the Elders had obtained a more complete copy it, and if he and Brijit were somehow implicated.

Because an intact version of the text had never been found, it was believed that one did not exist. As Weylon understood it, all the Elders had was bits and pieces of the writing.

If a complete version of the Prophecy ever was found Weylon could guess that the Elders would be very invested in it. A complete copy of the Prophecy would change life in Séreméla and all of Five Corners. He was sure some of the Elders would not welcome such a thing.

If the princess was carrying a girl-child, then both her life and that of her child could be in danger. That combined with the prospect of the lost text of the Prophecy being found meant they were in for some very turbulent years.

Weylon looked over to where Brijit was sleeping. She was moaning softly in her sleep. His brow furrowed. Brijit had told him about the dreams that she had started to have several months ago. They were complex and frightening, and she didn't know what they meant, if anything. Weylon didn't believe in dreams meaning much of anything. He thought the magik wielders put too much stock into such things. He believed what he could feel and touch, not abstract things.

Still he didn't like to see Brijit so upset. Since the incident with Ana and her baby, Brijit had been dreaming more and more. She had woken up screaming almost nightly, and Weylon had noticed that it was becoming more and more difficult for her to fall asleep at night. She rode silently throughout the day with dark circles under her worried eyes.

As her whimpering grew louder, Weylon moved closer to Brijit. Instinctively he reached out and began to rub her back. "It's okay, Brij," he murmured softly, knowing that she was fast asleep and wouldn't be able to feel or hear him. But after a few minutes her restlessness ceased, and she fell back into a deep sleep.

Weylon forced himself to move back to his side of the fire. He couldn't let himself develop feelings for Brijit. To do so would take his attention off his duties as *Coimirceoirí.* And yet he couldn't deny that he worried about her. The more he learned of her, the more he realized how important she was to the Elders, and that scared him for her sake. He had started to wonder if the "fact" of him being the most gifted *Coimirceoirí* in half a century hadn't been planted to take the attention off Brijit. Her gifts as an empath were stronger than any he had ever seen or heard of. And yet there had to be more to make her so valuable to the Elders. But what it was he couldn't say. As he watched her sleep, he couldn't help wondering if there were secrets she was still hiding from him.

#

Brijit woke feeling more refreshed than she had in days. She looked over to where Weylon was packing up his belongings. No matter how late she fell asleep or how early she woke, he always seemed to be up before her.

And she had not been sleeping well. The farther they traveled from the Academy, the more Brigit's dreams were filled with dark shadows and growling animals, the likes of which she'd never seen before. The previous evening had been the first good night of sleep that she'd had since leaving the house where Ana and her child had died.

"Did you sleep well?" Weylon asked, his brown eyes filled with concern.

Brijit nodded and hurried out of her sleeping roll. She began to pack up her things. The Elder knights would arrive at any moment, and she wanted to make sure she was ready to leave. They never said much, but on the few occasions when she had still been in her sleeping roll when they had arrived, they had loomed over her, making her feel vulnerable and exposed as she packed up her things.

Having finished cleaning up their camp already, Weylon came over to help her with her packing.

"No bad dreams?" he asked, his face creased with concern.

Brijit shook her head. Surprisingly, her night had been calm and peaceful, free from the nightmares that had been plaguing her.

Weylon smiled, his brown eyes lighting up with relief. “Good, you needed the sleep.”

Brijit felt her cheeks heating. Weylon had been smiling more and more lately. Really smiling. She hadn’t thought it was possible when she’d first met him, he’d been so growly. But they had become much more like partners since Ana’s death.

She’d also noticed that Weylon was protective of her. Once she had thrown aside her act of ignorance and Weylon had opened up to her, things had shifted between them. This hadn’t gone unnoticed by the Elders, who now watched them with suspicion and a hint of disapproval. Brijit didn’t care. The more she discovered about the Elders’ world, the more she realized she needed an ally.

She didn’t trust the Elders at all. She couldn’t help feeling that both Weylon and her were pawns in a game they didn’t understand. She knew Weylon felt the same way.

After Ana’s death, Brijit told him about the letter she had found and what it had revealed about their journey. She also told him what Serena and Elsa had overheard. Weylon’s expression had darkened when Brijit mentioned the Prophecy. When she asked him about it, he had told her all he knew about the strange religion some of the Elders followed. Part of Brijit was fascinated to hear about this part of the Elders’ culture that she had been unaware of. But another part of her was irritated by the omission of this knowledge by the Academy. Clearly, there was much Brijit still had to learn about the Elders and their world.

Shaking her head, Brijit realized she’d been lost in her thoughts. Without a word, Weylon had saddled her horse and was tying her saddlebag behind her mount.

Brijit walked over to him and smiled apologetically as she stroked the horse's neck. "I'm sorry. I seem to be slow at getting going this morning."

Weylon smiled down at her and reached out and touched her cheek. Warmth rushed to where his fingers ran over her skin. Brijit refrained from leaning into his hand. "It's okay, you needed the rest."

She looked up him, noticing how handsome he was now that he had dropped the stern mask he had been wearing for so long. He was looking down at her, and Brijit was surprised at the emotion she saw in his eyes. She lifted her shielding completely and sent to him her feelings. But he didn't look surprised, he already knew how she was feeling about him.

"Brijit," Weylon stepped closer to her, bending his head.

Brijit instinctively raised her chin and closed her eyes, waiting for his lips to touch her own. But instead he pulled away, stepping around her.

"We are ready to go." Weylon's tone was gruff and distant as he spoke to the Elder knights who had appeared on the side of the camp.

Brijit's cheeks heated and her heart pounded. Had the Elders seen them? She bit her lip and squeezed her eyes shut. *Coimirceoirí* were forbidden to have relationships. If the Elders had arrived and caught them kissing, she didn't know what would happen. Weylon walked past her to get to his horse, his eyes meeting hers. They said everything. Be careful, Brijit, be careful.

#

The farther west they traveled, the wilder the land became. For the last two days they had been riding through a dark and overgrown forest that had a sinister feel to it. The trees seemed to close in on them. At times Brijit felt as if the very air was being sucked from her lungs.

Instinctively, she stayed close to Weylon throughout the trek through the black trees. The ground was a dead gray color, and the air spelled faintly of sulfur and rot. The small animals, that had been numerous in the woods at the start of their journey, had all but disappeared. The deeper they went into the dying woods, the more nauseated Brijit felt. Her stomach protested continually. Even the thought of food made her retch.

The supplies they had collected at the market by the inn were all but gone now. Weylon had boasted of his skill in hunting at the beginning of their trip, but he had not caught any fresh game for the last day and half. They were surviving on the roots and fruit that Brijit had collected before they entered the dying wood, along with the last of the dried meat and cheese Weylon had bought before they left the village.

The Elders disappeared into the dying trees more and more, leaving Weylon and Brijit alone.

"I hate this place," she said to Weylon on their second night making camp.

He looked around and then came and sat near her on the log he'd moved near the fire. Their fire itself had been difficult to light with all the wood saturated with the mist that never seemed to disappear. After Weylon had coaxed it to life, it had still flickered weakly in the damp air.

Brijit found herself inching closer to Weylon, her body automatically craving the heat that seemed to radiate from him. He reached out and put his arm around her shoulders and Brijit gave in to her need for human contact, letting her head fall to his shoulder.

"We must be in the heart of Jirgen Forest now," he noted.

Brijit remembered where the forest had been drawn on the Elder man. She wondered how much farther it would be to Tèarmann.

"What do you know of Tèarmann?" she asked.

Weylon shook his head. "I believe it's an ancient Elder fortress. But I thought that it was just a ruin now, not an inhabitable building."

The Rift had been clearly labeled on the map, along with the Dead Sea. Brijit remembered that the fortress was on the very edge of The Rift.

"Do you still think that's where we are going?" she asked.

Weylon stared into the dying forest around them, considering. Then he nodded. “It makes sense. It’s the only thing between here and The Rift itself.”

Brijit shivered as she looked at the dying trees surrounding their camp.

“Nothing can grow here. It is an extension of The Rift.” Weylon said before pausing and looking around. “Rumors are that the evil from The Rift is oozing into the land. The Elders don’t know how to handle it. They are taking their commands from the council, but what they need is a real leader. That’s why the birth of the child the princess is carrying is so important. If it is indeed a girl, as the whispers have proclaimed, then she will be the next ruler of Séremęla.”

“And how will a child save Five Corners from The Rift?” Brijit asked looking around at the desolation that surrounded them.

Brijit could feel Weylon shake his head as she rested her own aching head on his shoulder. “I don’t know. But the legends say the girl-child will save her people.”

Brijit nodded. She had heard similar stories told at the Academy. While the instructors were never up front with what the Elders really wanted, there had been the History of Elder Society classes, and everyone knew about the Elders’ desire for a girl ruler to take up the legendary Queen Aibhilín’s mantle.

She remembered how brutally the Elders had killed the child in the village and wondered if the royal child could be in as much danger. It seemed a strange thought, but at the same time it was not outside the realm of possibilities. Nothing was as they knew it. And the farther they traveled from the Academy the more Brijit knew she didn’t understand the land she had grown up in – at all. Looking around her now, it was clear that this forest would never recover from the sickness that engulfed it. Pain exploded in her head, as it had been doing off and on all day. She lowered her head to Weylon's shoulder and closed her eyes.

"Do you have any idea what the Prophecy they speak of contains, Weylon?" Brijit tried to remember what the letter she had read had said, but she couldn't.

Weylon sighed. "I thought it was just another rumor. I didn't even know if it actually existed. But the story I heard says the Elders supposedly have several scraps of an old parchment that predicts the future." He snorted. "I don't particularly believe in fortune telling, but some of the Elders give credence to the whole thing. They believe it religiously – so much so that they have been prone to violence in the past when confronted with their beliefs."

Brijit's stomach suddenly cramped and she bent forward, her breath taken away.

"Are you all right?" Weylon's voice was filled with concern.

"I'm just not feeling very well," she whispered.

She knew Weylon was studying her closely. "Again. This is happening too much, Brijit. You need to eat something."

Brijit felt bile rising in her throat. She had the urge to pull away from him, but then he started to rub her back gently and the motion comforted her in a strange way. "No," she said weakly. "I don't think I can."

"Here I'll put your roll near the fire at least. Then maybe you'll warm up a bit."

He set about making a bed for her as close to the weak flames as possible.

"Lie down and perhaps you will feel better after you rest."

Brijit lay on her side, curled in a ball, praying that the cramps would go away. She'd not felt so sick since she was a child of eight and she'd eaten some berries her grandmother had collected to make medicine with. Her grandmother had laughed at her and scolded her at the same time.

"You've learned your lesson, child. Thankfully the sickness you feel will pass soon. If you'd eaten those mushrooms," she'd pointed to a pile of fungus she'd also collected, "I'm afraid I would have lost you."

But Brijit hadn't eaten anything in the last twenty-four hours and before that it had only been the food that she had prepared herself with supplies they had obtained outside the Dead Zone. She didn't understand why she was feeling so ill. She had tried to combat the cramps with ginger root, but the herb had done little to ease her suffering. For some reason she felt it was important to hide her condition from the Elders, which had made traveling even more miserable than usual.

Weylon sat on the log keeping watch over her.

After an intolerable hour, the pains eased a bit.

"Have you tried shielding yourself?" Weylon asked suddenly.

Brijit looked over at him blearily. Since she had shared what she knew with Weylon, she hadn't felt the need to shield herself. Why would he even suggest such a thing?

"This place is filled with evil. Surely you can feel it."

She nodded. The darkness in the forest was overwhelming.

"You are so open, Brijit, like a sponge. Have you considered that the powers that are draining this place might be having the same effect on you?"

Brijit thought about it. She supposed it might be possible that what was killing the vegetation and driving the animals away was affecting her. But the thought of shielding herself against her setting seemed overwhelming, and she was so weak she didn't know if she would have the energy to do so.

"I don't know," she whispered truthfully.

"Are you well enough to try the centering exercise?"

Weylon had showed her how to focus her energy inward, thus blocking any outward influence. While she was gifted at shielding, she rarely practiced any exercises to help her with it – she had never needed to. Weylon had told her about the grounding and centering work they had engaged in at Stone Mountain. Curious, Brijit had asked him to walk her through one of the exercises. She was surprised when she found that shielding came even easier to her after she had finished the exercise.

Even though she was weak right now, too weak to attempt shielding herself from her setting, Brijit nodded at Weylon's suggestion. She had to do something if she was going to get through this forest to the fortress on the other side. She didn't know how long she would last if the nausea didn't disappear. Slowly she sat up.

Weylon reached into his pouch and pulled out a crystal she had never seen before. She looked at him questioningly.

"I was given this by my old teacher when I was very young. Focusing on it will help you to gain control. It's a talisman, something to ground your meditation."

Brijit nodded and stared at the blue-green crystal Weylon placed on the blanket before her. Then she began breathing deeply.

She tried the visualization he'd shown her before. Creating a crystal bubble around her that was impermeable by any outside influence.

After some time, Brijit opened her eyes. The feeling of sickness had disappeared.

She looked at Weylon and smiled. "That was amazing," she said as she handed him the crystal.

"Keep it," he told her, as he reached out and captured her hand in his own, effectively closing her fingers around the small rock. They stood like that for a minute, his hand swallowing her smaller one with the crystal inside, staring into one another's eyes. Brijit felt caught, frozen in a web she didn't understand. Then Weylon let go of her hand and stepped away.

"I don't feel right taking it," she said once she found her voice.

Weylon turned back to her and shook his head. "I don't need it any more. It will help you until you've mastered your practice, especially while we are here and your energy is being sucked away by the evil." He stared hard at her for a long moment. "To be honest, I suspect you are going to need to practice far more than I do."

Brijit looked at him questioningly, wondering what he knew, but he turned his back on her. What did that mean? Did Weylon have suspicions as to what her role was in helping the Elders? If so, why hadn't he told her. They were so open with one another now, Brijit was surprised he would keep his suspicions to himself. Unless he suspected something she wouldn't like. Regardless he should tell her his suspicions. But before she could ask him, he changed the subject. She let it go.

"Now are you hungry?"

She considered how her stomach felt and was surprised when it actually growled in hunger.

"I am." She moved to stand, but Weylon waved her back to her bedroll.

"Take it easy there. You might be feeling better but you still look inordinately pale. I can handle getting us some food."

Brijit watched as Weylon moved over to their packs and began to retrieve various food stuffs. She wondered what he was going to make for their evening meal. While she had done most of the cooking thus far, when Weylon put together a meal it usually focused on dried meat and cheese. Despite her hunger, she didn't think she'd be able to handle meat at present.

"What are you going to make?" she asked, unable to resist.

"It's a surprise," he said in a teasing voice, as he turned to the ingredients he had spread on the blanket in front of him. Brijit craned her neck to see what he had there, but he scolded her, "No peeking. Don't you trust me to make something that is edible?"

"I'm not sure!" she jibbed back.

He looked over to her with an expression of mock pain on his face. "I'm hurt," he said melodramatically.

Brijit couldn't help grinning at his teasing manner. It had been this way lately, when he relaxed, Weylon was actually fun to be around. Brijit settled back on her blankets.

As Weylon bent his head back to the task at hand, a black shape suddenly burst from the trees behind him. The creature was on him in less than a second, its tarry black fur matted and its red eyes wild and ferocious. Brijit reached into her boot for her dagger but before she could react, the creature had sunk its razor-sharp ebony teeth into Weylon's side.

"No!" Brijit's scream echoed through the empty forest. She had never seen a creature like the one that had Weylon in its grasp. It was jet black, with those eerie red eyes rolling in its head. Its snarls were guttural.

Weylon had his own dagger out and had buried it to the hilt in the creature's shoulder to little effect. The monster continued to gnaw on Weylon's side, almost as if it were feeding. Blood soaked Weylon's shirt and leather pants, pooling in a dark puddle beneath him. But he was still fighting the creature, plunging his dagger into it again and again. The creature growled and continued to feast.

It was obvious that Weylon would be dead if she didn't do something. Her dagger would obviously be of little use. Brijit looked around the clearing for a weapon and saw Weylon's sword in a pile beside their packs.

She moved to retrieve it, not knowing if she was even strong enough to lift the huge broad sword when the trees parted. Beriadan and the two Elder knights broke into the clearing. One cocked an arrow and let it fly before Brijit could say a word.

She watched in horror, terrified that the arrow would hit Weylon who was in the creature's grip. But the arrow buried itself in the creature's side, to little effect. The Elder didn't hesitate but release three more arrows in the creature before it dropped Weylon.

Beriadan sprinted to where the creature was and drew his sword. As the creature hissed and snarled at him, he severed its head from its body.

Brijit was frozen, staring at the head that rolled toward her. The snarl was still on its face, eyes wide open and filled with evil. Brijit stepped back, horror making her dumb.

"Healer, get over here," Beriadan commanded.

Brijit ripped her gaze away from those red eyes. She looked over to where Weylon had collapsed on the ground, blood making a red pool beneath him. Fear gripped her and she ran over to him.

"Weylon," she gasped as she fell to her knees.

"I'm all right," he said softly to her, but his face was gray. Blood was everywhere. Brijit choked back a sob and forced herself to smile at him.

"Of course, you're all right. Just a little scratch," she joked, her voice coming out broken and raspy. "But maybe I should see if I can stop the bleeding."

Weylon smiled faintly and nodded.

Brijit pulled up his shirt and saw the bite wound. Her heart sank when she saw how deep the creature's teeth had penetrated his skin. But she kept her face clear of all emotion.

"I need to reach into your mind," she said softly. "May I?"

Brijit always asked before she probed a patient's mind.

Weylon nodded.

Brijit reached out and at first found herself overwhelmed with emotions. She tried to wade through them, focusing on pain. She ignored the fact that she'd thought Weylon was void of feeling for so long and now she'd found that he seemed to be overwhelmed by it. Focusing her mind, she found the pain center in his mind and sent soothing thoughts to it.

She had no medicine that would ease this pain; the mind link was better than nothing.

One of the Elders brought her the medicine kit she had packed. Brijit nodded her thanks and reached into the bag, removing linen bandages.

"I need to clean the wound, Weylon," she said softly as she took a small piece of linen and soaked it in the antiseptic mixture Raspella had packed in her kit. "This will sting."

Weylon groaned and bucked as she wiped the blood away from the wound. Brijit gasped when she saw what was under the blood.

"What is it?" asked Beriadan.

Brijit stared. "I don't know. I've never seen anything like this," she murmured.

The puncture wounds were surrounded with rings of black and the darkness was radiating outward. Brijit let go of the pain control she was holding in her mind, and Weylon screamed. She quickly re-established it.

She looked up at Beriadan. "I don't know what this is. I don't know what medicines to use."

One of the other Elders approached to take a look. He immediately unsheathed his sword. "*Aptrgangr*," he hissed, staring at the wound in horror. Beriadan looked at him, shock registering on his face as he realized his fellow Elder was right. The Elder moved toward Weylon, his intention clear.

Brijit threw herself across Weylon's body. "No! You will not hurt him," she screamed at the Elder.

"You don't know what you are saying, *Coimirceoirí*," Beriadan told her. "If he has been attacked by an *Aptrgangr* – and I don't doubt my comrade, who has seen this kind of wound before – he will die, and it won't be a kind death. Let us do it swiftly."

Brijit met Weylon's eyes and saw that they were full of fear. "I won't let them take you," she whispered. "I will save you."

Weylon shook his head slightly, but he was too weak to speak.

"I *will*," Brijit repeated.

"How can you heal one that has been bitten by an *Aptrgangr*?" Beriadan asked.

Brijit raised her chin, looking at him defiantly. "I don't know," she admitted.

Beriadan looked at her coldly. "Well, you better figure it out, Healer. If not, he will be dead within a day, and it won't be an easy death."

#

Brijit treated Weylon with the herbs and treatments she had in her bag, but nothing was making a difference. His entire right side was now black, and he'd lost consciousness, which meant that she could let go of the mental pain control she was holding.

It had been exhausting holding the pain at arm's length, so Brijit was relieved when Weylon finally succumbed to sleep, but she was also growing increasingly worried that he would not wake again.

"Please, Weylon," she whispered. "I don't know what to do. Please don't leave me alone."

But he didn't respond. His had grown grayer than before, and the black had started streaking up his neck and down his leg. The poison, or whatever it was, was moving fast.

Brijit was becoming more and more frantic. She had no idea what to do. The Elders had not left her; they were standing guard in the camp, but they did not help her. Brijit didn't know if it was because they didn't know how to help or if this was some kind of elaborate test of her skills. Either way, she was becoming increasingly frustrated. Tears filled her eyes.

She went over her training. There was nothing she could remember about such an injury. In fact, she'd never heard of such a thing. Festering poison from a large beast was unheard of. She'd treated poisonous bites from spiders, snakes and occasionally scorpions, but nothing on the scale of the beast that had attacked Weylon. She didn't even know such creatures could be venomous. Anger infused her for a few minutes. Why had Raspella left such an important part of her training undeveloped? They had never even discussed a wound such as this one.

Unless Raspella hadn't ever heard of a wound like this one. Brijit closed her eyes, frustrated tears burning behind the lids. What was she going to do?

And suddenly an idea came to her. An old idea.

There was one healer who was more gifted than any other she had known. Her grandmother. But getting to her grandmother was unthinkable. She had no idea how many days' journey it would be to her grandmother's home, and it was obvious that Weylon wouldn't survive even a short trip. He was beyond being moved already.

Desperate Brijit reached up and grasped the pendant at her neck. Her grandmother had given it to her before she left to study at the Academy.

Brijit remembered it clearly. That had not been a happy parting. Her grandmother had originally been furious with Brijit for choosing to become Coimirceoirí. But as she accepted the fact that her granddaughter was going to leave with or without her blessing, her anger had been displaced by resignation and sadness. She didn't understand why Brijit was so entranced with the idea of becoming a *Coimirceoirí* to the Elders. Her grandmother had been a village wise woman her entire life. She assumed Brijit would want to follow in her footsteps.

Now Brijit wondered if her grandmother had seen her granddaughter as turning her back on the *Kurunii* and choosing the *Coimirceoirí* over her heritage? But Grandmamma had never told Brijit the truth about their family. Even in the end.

Her grandmother's disappointment had weighed heavy on Brijit's heart in the days leading up to her departure. But on her last evening at home, her grandmother had come to her chamber.

"Brijit, you know I do not approve of what you are doing. I see only misery in your future. The path you are choosing leads clearly to tragedy." Her grandmother reached out and touched her arm. "I would wish to protect you from such a path, but I also see that this is impossible. Your mind has been made and with that your fate has been sealed. I do love you, child, don't ever forget that."

At that, Brijit had burst into tears and her grandmother had gathered her into her arms and held her tight. "Don't cry, my child," she had soothed. "It is as it shall be."

She had pulled away then and unhooked the chain that she always wore around her neck.

"I will not see you again in the living world," she said, and Brijit immediately protested.

"Grandmamma, don't say that."

But her grandmother cut her off, her dark eyes sharp. "Don't interrupt, child," she scolded. "We can't deny what the fates have ruled to be the truth even if it is something we would not wish to hear. You understand this?"

Brijit nodded reluctantly.

"Good. Then I have taught you something valuable." She put the pendant into Brijit's hand. "We shall not meet again in the living world but I will always be with you. Wear this pendant always. Keep it close to your heart and out of sight at all times, Brijit." Her grandmother embraced her again, her arms squeezing Brijit tightly. "Remember me, child. In your time of greatest need, you will know how to reach out to me."

Her grandmother pulled away and grasped both of Brijit's hands and looked deep into her eyes. Brijit started to tremble and wanted to pull away, but her grandmother held her in a grip so tight it was impossible to break.

Then she hugged her granddaughter close. "I have told you something very important, child. You will carry it in your deepest heart. And remember to keep that pendant close and out of sight."

The memory surfaced in Brijit's mind so clearly and suddenly that before she could even think about what she was doing, she had removed the pendant her grandmother had given her and held it in front of her eyes.

The silver triquetra cradled within a circle. The symbol her friends had said could only be worn by descendants of *Kurunii*. Brijit closed her eyes. It was the one thing she had not told Weylon about. Something had told her to keep that knowledge close to her heart until the time was right.

She opened her eyes and looked behind her in the clearing. Beriadan did not seem at all surprised to see the triquetra in her hands. Something shifted in Brijit as she realized he had known all along. He knew more than she did about what she was; perhaps that was why he had allowed her to attempt to heal Weylon rather than killing him outright.

Pushing the thought aside, Brijit focused on the pendant. She began to breathe and meditate on her grandmother. She stared at the pendant, willing her grandmother to come to her. Her eyes drifted shut.

#

"Brijit. Open your eyes child."

Brijit opened her eyes and found herself sitting on a stool in her grandmother's kitchen. A soup pot was simmering over the fire and the old yellow tabby cat, Rufus, was sleeping in the corner. The familiar hominess of the scene brought tears to her eyes.

"Grandmamma?" she whispered, wondering if she'd slipped into a dream. Rufus lifted his head and lazily leapt down from his cushion. He prowled over to Brijit, looked up at her pensively, blinked his green eyes three times and then jumped into her lap. He turned in a circle, digging his claws into her thighs until she cried out, then he curled into a ball and began to purr. Slowly, his eyes closed and he went back to sleep.

Her grandmother was bundling herbs for drying on her counter. She looked up at Brijit and smiled.

"I knew you'd figure it out sooner or later."

Brijit shook her head in confusion.

"The pendant is a talisman," her grandmother explained.

She started at the word. It was the second time today that she'd heard someone use it. She thought of Weylon's crystal. Now she was here with her grandmother she had to question why he had a magikal item? Where had Weylon come by such a thing and how had he learned to wield it?

Her grandmother laughed. Had it always sounded that much like a cackle?

"A talisman is a powerful thing, Grandmamma."

She looked over at Brijit, her black eyes even darker than normal. "It is," the old woman acknowledged.

Brijit felt a shiver race down her spine.

"All magik can be a dark thing, my child. Have they taught you nothing that that precious Academy of yours." The distaste in her grandmother's tone was palatable. She pinned Brijit with her eyes. "But you have sought me out for a different reason."

Brijit was brought back to the present. Weylon was dying as she was in this vision or whatever it was.

She nodded.

"What help do you seek from me?"

"My traveling companion is dying. I don't know what to do," Brijit burst out, not bothering with long explanation.

"You mean the *Coimirceoirí* who is traveling with you." Her grandmother paused in her work and looked at Brijit critically. "Are you certain saving him is such a wise choice?"

Shock caused Brijit to lose her breath for a moment. Regardless of her grandmother's feelings about the *Coimirceoirí*, it wasn't like her to wish one dead.

"Why would you say that, Grandmamma?"

Her grandmother didn't answer but went back to her herbs.

"The poison will not be easy to stop," she murmured, and Brijit felt frustration building within her.

"I know that but there must be something –"

"Oh, there is something," her grandmother cut her off. "But once the poison has entered a person, it is impossible to completely eradicate. I suppose they didn't teach you about the bite of the *Aptrgangr* at your Academy, either?" Her grandmother's voice rose in anger. "Saving your friend is foremost in your mind right now but what happens when that poison continues to eat away at him, for years down the road."

Brijit shook her head. No, it couldn't be true. Her grandmother had to be mistaken. What she was saying meant Weylon was already lost to her, but she refused to believe it was true. Brijit throat closed, threatening to choke her. "Are you certain that will happen?"

Her grandmother looked at her closely.

"Is there another reason you wish to save this boy, Brijit?" Her grandmother's tone sharpened with suspicion as her dark eyes narrowed. "Have you gone so far from your training as to develop feelings for him?" The distain in her voice hit Brijit like a slap.

Brijit felt her cheeks redden.

"No," she denied.

"No?" her grandmother raised her white eyebrows and looked at her skeptically. "Your words sound false to me. Are you being honest with yourself, my granddaughter?"

Brijit stood up angrily. Rufus fell the floor with an angry snarl.

"I don't have time for this. Weylon is dying. Can you help me or not, Grandmamma?"

Her grandmother looked hard at her.

"So this is the way it is," she said after a few moments. Her shoulders slumped in defeat, then she began to chant quietly to herself. Brijit watched her, feeling ill as the woman who raised her continued to recite incantations that Brijit knew had to be invoking her dark magik. But Brijit didn't care – she would do anything to save Weylon.

"In the dead forest, you will find a red mushroom growing. Take three of them. No more, no less. Brew them over your fire until the broth turns golden. Too long and it will be ineffective; too short and it will kill him. But he is dying anyway. So I wouldn't worry too much."

Brijit breathed out in relief, suddenly realizing that she had been holding her breath for too long. She hadn't been sure her grandmother was going to help her after all.

"But Brijit," the old woman said.

She looked at her grandmother.

"Be sure this is what you want, my child. Choices you make now will affect the destiny of your life in this realm."

A sudden sense of foreboding filled Brijit. Her grandmother was always talking in riddles. What could she mean? Weylon's groan suddenly filled the small house. Brijit could feel herself being pulled from the vision.

"Your choice is made. We shall not see one another again." Her grandmother bowed her head. "I love you, my child. Be at peace."

As her grandmother and her house began to fade from view, Brijit could hear Rufus hissing and yowling. And then she was back in the camp, with Weylon tossing violently on the sleeping roll in front of her.

#

Two of the Elder knights stayed with Weylon while Beriadan accompanied Brijit into the forest. The vision of her grandmother was still with her, making Brijit tremble slightly. She could feel the pendant hanging heavily between her breasts where she had tucked it back inside her tunic, still out of sight even though she knew the Elders had seen her use it.

Her eyes scoured the ground looking for the red mushrooms her grandmother had said would heal Weylon. Not cure him completely but heal him. She hadn't given up on a cure but for now she would be satisfied with healing.

Her grandmother's words haunted her, and yet the urgency to do something to save Weylon's life took precedence over the old woman's warnings.

It was clear that Weylon was nearing the point of no return. He had been thrashing violently on the bedroll when she left him. His gray skin filled with a webbing of black veins. Brijit feared that even if she found the mushroom her grandmother had talked of, by the time she prepared the brew it would be far too late for Weylon.

"Time is ebbing, Healer," Beriadan suddenly said, voicing her worries aloud. "I fear you may not be able to save him."

Suddenly a patch of red near the exposed roots of a dying tree caught her attention.

"There!" Brijit pointed and sprinted to where the mushrooms were growing. They seemed to glow iridescently, as if they were from another world. Gingerly she reached down and picked three of them. The rest of the fungus instantly vanished and Brijit gasped. But the three vibrant-colored stalks in her hand remained.

Shaking off the strangeness, Brijit made her way back to camp with Beriadan. Weylon looked much the same as when they had left him, but his groans were becoming louder by the second. Ignoring his increasing moans, Brijit set to brewing the mushrooms as her grandmother had instructed. The Elders didn't question her. They left her to her work.

Brijit watched the brew closely and was surprised at how quickly the fungus broke down. She kept stirring it, remembering the instructions her grandmother gave her. She was used to making tinctures and other remedies. She had trained for years doing this and had been the best student at the Academy. If ever there was a time to put her skill set to work, it was now.

As she watched, the brew turned a soft yellow color, not yet golden. She kept stirring and pondering her grandmother's words. She was shocked that the old woman had suggested she might leave Weylon for dead. Her grandmother, while she acknowledged that death did happen, always fought hard for her patients, particularly young ones. It went against the grain for her to suggest that one should die. What that could mean filled Brijit with a sense of terror that she didn't want to examine too closely.

But what else had Grandmamma said? That the poison would never leave Weylon. Brijit looked around the forest, noting the dying trees. This had not happened quickly. Could a similar thing happen to a person if they were infected as the forest had clearly been? The thought was terrifying. What about the creature that had attacked Weylon? Brijit could not help wondering what it had been before it had become the evil beast that she had seen. She looked over to where its body lay on the ground and shuddered.

It was impossible to think that Weylon could become like that. Her grandmother must be mistaken.

The broth started to turn from yellow to a deep gold. Brijit held her breath and stirred it three more times and then removed it from the heat. She poured it into a wooden bowl and then looked over at Beriadan.

"I will need you to hold him still, while I try to get some of this down his throat."

Beriadan nodded and came over to where Weylon lay on the ground. Suddenly Weylon's eyes flew open, and he snarled at Beriadan, striking out with his arms.

The Elder seemed unperturbed by Weylon's aggressive response. He easily pinned Weylon to the ground.

Beriadan looked at Brijit. "This is the best you will get. Try not to drown him."

Irritation prickled at Brijit, but she knew better than to argue with Beriadan. She knelt beside Weylon.

"Weylon, this will help."

He snarled at her, spittle gathering at the corners of his now black lips. Brijit swallowed hard. This had to be done.

She took a spoonful of the liquid and tried to put it in his mouth, but Weylon spat it out at her.

"They will win," he hissed, his eyes rolling manically. "They will win. They are coming, and you all will bow to them."

Brijit looked at Beriadan, who shook his head at her.

She was not going to get any of the remedy into Weylon while he was in this state. Desperate, Brijit reached out for his mind as she'd done earlier, hoping to be able to send calming thoughts to him. But she gasped as the darkness engulfed her. *Come play with us, little one.* The voices filled her head. We like the innocent like you. *Come along, he has led us right to you. Be our plaything while you can last.*

Brijit tried to sever the connection but found she was held firm to Weylon's diseased mind. Try as she might, she couldn't let go. Blind fear overtook her, and she began to fight in earnest.

Breathing hard, she pushed against the veil of darkness that was covering her eyes and saw Weylon's face. In desperation, she took the bowl and held it to his lips. She poured all the contents down his throat, ignoring his choking and what splattered down his chin. She kept pouring until it was gone, her only aim to break free of the evilness that had filled her thoughts.

The darkness engulfed her mind and then suddenly she was thrown back on the ground.

Brijit lay there, looking at Beriadan in dismay. Weylon began convulsing violently and then lay still, not breathing. She knew now what her grandmother had been trying to tell her. Weylon was beyond her help. And as she stared at his lifeless form in front her, she knew she had failed.

Chapter Ten

Beriadan stared at Brijit.

"You have killed him," he said.

The two other Elders crossed the clearing to where Weylon was lying and looked down.

Brijit sobbed quietly. She may have killed Weylon, but after being in his mind she couldn't help wondering if he were better off dead. No one should have to live in the grip of such darkness.

"He is not dead."

Brijit looked up blindly through her tears. The second Elder knight was looking down at Weylon, his eyes alit with interest.

Almost against her will, Brijit looked over. What she saw was unbelievable. The black veins below Weylon's skin were receding, and his color, while still gray, wasn't as pale as before. As Brijit watched, his chest began to rise and fall. He was, indeed, alive.

"Well done, Healer. Well done."

Brijit nodded. But as she watched life returning to Weylon, her grandmother's warning returned to her and her heart began to fill with fear. She asked herself, *What have I done?*

#

Brijit worried they would be stuck in the Dead Zone until Weylon recovered enough to travel, but the Elders surprised her by putting him on a horse the very day after the attack.

"We cannot linger here," Beriadan told her when she protested.

"But he is not in any way fit to be moved yet. You wanted me to save him, but what you are suggesting will kill him."

He ignored her completely and continued to prepare for departure. When they lifted Weylon's now unconscious body to his horse, he threatened to slide off the other side.

"See, he can't sit up."

"He doesn't have to," Beriadan told her, and he proceeded to tie Weylon to his saddle. "We cannot linger here," he repeated, his green eyes nervously shifting to the dying trees surrounding them. "We have been in this forest too long already."

Brijit followed his gaze and felt a darkness enter her heart. Beriadan was right. They needed to leave.

They tied Weylon's horse to the back of Beriadan's and then set a brisk pace that had Brijit's teeth chattering. She didn't want to think about how badly Weylon was being jarred on the back of his mount. A part of her was grateful for the Elders' pace.

When they finally stopped for a rest, she was dismayed to see blood running down Weylon's side again. The riding had reopened his wound. While the wound was troubling, Brijit was relieved to see that his blood was red and healthy looking. Only a small bit of the foul black discharge remained. He was still unconscious, thankfully. Brijit didn't want to re-enter his mind, even in the name of pain control. At least not for some time.

After she had redressed Weylon's wound, she suggested they break for the day, pointing out that more riding would just aggravate the bleeding. Beriadan was adamant in his refusal.

"You have ensured that he will not die from his wounds. Now we must ensure that we get out of this forest before the rest of us succumb."

Her experiences of the previous day had left her shaken and exhausted. She rode automatically, thankful that the Elders' horses were so accommodating to their riders.

Brijit had no choice but to follow the Elders far into the night. Finally, under a full moon, they broke from the forest and emerged in a desert where no vegetation at all grew. Brijit was so tired she feared that she would fall from her saddle, and she was relieved when the Elders halted, once they'd left the dead wood some distance behind.

"We will rest here until the sun rises. But that is all," she was told. "If you need sleep, I would suggest you take it now."

Brijit did just that, pulling out her sleeping roll and collapsing into it. She marveled at how the Elders themselves did not seem to need any sleep. She remembered Weylon saying that they weren't human so they didn't need rest in the same way, but she didn't dwell on that thought for long. A black, dreamless sleep soon overtook her, and before she knew it she was being shaken awake.

She changed Weylon's dressing and was happy to see that the bleeding had, for the most part, stopped. The blackness that had originally oozed from the wound had also decreased. Now there was just the faintest ring of black around each of the puncture marks.

When she mounted her horse, Brijit was surprised to see how far the desert stretched. As far as she could see in every direction, there was nothing but dull brown sand. The dead forest had been swallowed up by the night, and she could not guess the direction they had come from the previous evening.

It was early afternoon when something finally appeared on the horizon. It looked like a massively tall structure. Brijit squinted into the distance but couldn't be sure.

As they got closer, Brijit saw that the building was a fortress of sorts. She realized that it must be Tèarmann, the fortress they had seen on the map. But this didn't look like the ruin Weylon had described. This was a working fortress, clearly maintained and used by the Elders. With a shiver, she wondered how close The Rift lay on the other side of the fortress.

They came to a twelve-foot-high stone wall that encircled the structure. Beriadan greeted the guards at the gates, who were obviously expecting them. They were led into the courtyard.

Weylon hadn't regained consciousness yet, and Brijit was starting to get worried. Would he ever wake? But even as she asked herself that question, part of her wondered if she wanted him to wake up.

The Elders dismounted. A stretcher was brought from the fortress by two young Elder men. A tall woman trailed them, giving instructions on how to unfasten Weylon from his mount.

"Tying him to his horse? Really, that was the best you could do, Beriadan?" the Elder woman turned on the knights, her dark green eyes blazing with anger. "You know better than to treat a patient like that!"

Beriadan stared at her stonily and then said, "We did what we had to in order to bring them here alive."

"Alive. Just barely. Yes, you did a good job of that. Next time perhaps we should specify in good health, as well." She didn't wait for a reply but motioned the young Elder men to carry Weylon inside.

Brijit scurried after them, hurrying to keep up and barely noticing the winding stone hallways that they strode down. Finally, they stopped and carried Weylon into a bedchamber that was both spacious and clean. A fire was already burning in the grate, and for the first time in a long time, Brijit felt the comforts of civilization wash over her. A wave of exhaustion hit her so hard she actually swayed on her feet.

"You can go and get some rest now, child. I can see to what he needs."

Brijit turned around in surprise and saw the Elder woman watching her. She was tall and Brijit could clearly see that she was very aged. Brijit couldn't help staring. She was the first Elder Brijit had ever seen who had lines on her face or showed any sign of aging at all.

The woman smiled at her, and Brijit realized that she had been staring too long.

"Truly, child, I can look after Weylon. You, Brijit, look dead on your feet."

Brijit froze, wondering how she knew their names but before she could ask, the woman moved to her side. Brijit instinctively blocked her access to Weylon, placing herself between his prone body and the Elder woman.

The older woman smiled at her. "We need to work together. We might as well start now."

Brijit just looked at her unmoving. There was no way she was going to leave Weylon alone with this Elder. Not after what had happened to Ana and her baby in that village. Not until she was sure she could trust her.

The woman sighed. "I suppose they've told you nothing?" She paused and studied Brijit for a few moments. "Of course they didn't. It is this ridiculous tradition to keep the *Coimirceoirí* in the dark. Well, I can't go against their wishes completely but they can't control what I tell you of myself."

She smiled encouragingly at Brijit. "I won't hurt Weylon. In fact, I am utterly not able to hurt a living being. I am Nestariel. I have many duties and roles to play. In time, you will learn of many of them. For now, you only need to know that I am a healer, like yourself."

Brijit looked at Nestariel for a long moment, still wondering if she could trust her. Could there be an Elder on their side? She wanted to think so, but she wasn't ready to believe it. She would start with something small and see how Nestariel reacted.

"I'll show you his wound," Brijit said and reached down to remove the dressing.

She heard Nestariel suck in her breath as she exposed Weylon's wound. Brijit was surprised. To her eyes the wound was looking much better.

The black circles around the puncture wounds were almost completely gone. Brijit was pleased with the progress, even though she was still concerned that he hadn't awoken yet.

She turned to Nestariel to ask her if she had any theories as to why Weylon was still unconscious and was surprised to see the horror on the Elder's ancient face.

"What did this to him?" An expression of fear and fascination lit up Nestariel's lined features.

"I'm not sure what it was. A creature from Jirgen Forest. It looked almost like a forest cat, but it was different, altered in some way."

Nestariel murmured something in the Elder language. "How is he still alive?" she asked, and Brijit recognized that anger was making her voice raspy. "What did you do to him?"

She stared at this Elder. Who was she to question her? Brijit had done what she could to save her fellow *Coimirceoirí*. She was a healer. Did the woman expect her to simply let him die?

She ignored the little voice inside that was reminding her she had been acting on more than duty when she had saved Weylon. She had been acting out of love.

Brijit pushed those thoughts aside. She wasn't ready to confront her own feelings yet, and she certainly couldn't let Nestariel even guess how close she had become to Weylon on their journey out.

When Brijit kept her lips pressed together, Nestariel sighed and then moderated her tone.

"Tell me, child, did you perform magik on him?"

"Magik?" Brijit asked vaguely. "No, I don't know how to do that."

Nestariel looked confused. "Then how did you manage this? No one can heal from a bite of the *Aptrgangr* without it."

Brijit shook her head. "I brewed him a healing tonic."

Nestariel turned and looked at her sharply. "Made from what?"

Brijit swallowed. “A red mushroom that grew in the forest.”

“Jirgen Forest? Nothing grows there.”

Brijit didn’t say anything.

“How did you know to find these mushrooms?” Nestariel asked, suddenly suspicious.

Brijit pressed her lips together. She didn’t know if it was wise to tell the healer about her communication with her grandmother.

Nestariel crossed her arms. “You’d best tell me so I can mitigate any damage that has been done.”

“No damage has been done. He was dying and the tonic saved him, just as Grandmamma said it would.”

Nestariel raised her eyebrows. “Your grandmother told you about these mushrooms? When? And more importantly, how?”

When Brijit didn’t answer, Nestariel grasped her by the shoulders in a grip far stronger than Brijit would have expected from such an old woman. She reached under Brijit’s tunic and found the pendant.

Her breath sucked in, and she dropped the pendant just as quickly as she had touched it.

“Ah, a triquetra. It begins to make sense.”

Brijit wondered what the old woman knew about the rune. She opened her mouth to ask but then closed it, not sure it was wise to trust this woman.

“You used this to visit your grandmother from the Jirgen Forest?” Nestariel asked.

Brijit nodded.

Nestariel shook her head and turned away.

“My grandmother gave it to me so I could contact her if I needed to.”

“Your grandmother is now dead.”

Brijit's heart stopped painfully as she remembered her grandmother's words. That she would not see Brijit again in the living world. "What?" How could Nestariel know such a thing? "No, I don't believe you."

The Elder turned back quickly and glared at Brijit. "If you contacted her from the Dead Zone with such a talisman, the evil from the forest would have found its way through the pendant and entered her home. If she is not dead yet, she soon will be."

Brijit remembered the hissing of Rufus as her vision ended and her grandmother's adamant statement that she would not see her in this realm again.

"No," Brijit whispered.

"I'm sorry," Nestariel softened slightly. "You could not have known it would happen, but your grandmother most likely did. She gave you that talisman to protect you, and she knew that if you used it in time of great need, then she ran the risk of losing her own life to whatever was threatening you. She obviously felt it was worth the risk."

Tears blurred Brijit's eyes as she thought of how selfless her grandmother had been for her entire life. She had let Brijit leave her even when it was not what her grandmother had wanted. She had helped her find a cure for Weylon even though she clearly thought it would be better for him to die. Her grandmother was the most giving person Brijit had ever met. And now…what had she done? Brijit collapsed onto the floor, her stomach churning with the knowledge that, if what Nestariel said were true, she had effectively killed her grandmother.

"You must grieve, child, but first you must tell me everything. I know it will be difficult, but I must know what your grandmother told you."

Brijit looked up at the Elder blearily, her mind racing with grief and shame.

Nestariel knelt beside her and took her face in her lined hands. "Brijit, it is important that you tell me this now. I can't help you or your friend unless I know the truth."

Brijit nodded. There was nothing she could do for her grandmother now but she could help Weylon.

"Grandmamma said the tonic would spare Weylon's life, but she also said it wouldn't remove all the poison from him. She warned me that saving him would mean that his life would forever be tainted by the darkness."

Nestariel narrowed her eyes. "So she knew that but she still told you how to save him." The Elder stood suddenly and began pacing. "Why would she do such a thing?"

Brijit knew. Her grandmother loved her and she had seen how important Weylon had become to her. But also her grandmother was essentially a healer at heart. She would never let any being die if she thought there was a possibility for them to live.

"I don't know. She just…my grandmother was a healer. If she could spare someone's life she would."

"At any cost?" Nestariel didn't wait for Brijit to answer. "Never mind." She waved her hand vaguely in front of her face and turned her attention back to where Weylon was lying on the bed. Then she stretched out her hand and helped Brijit to her feet. "How long has he been unconscious?"

Brijit swallowed. "Two days."

Nestariel nodded thoughtfully. "Then it is time he wakes. Let's see what damage has been done, shall we?"

Brijit's heart started to pound. She wasn't sure she was ready to see what Weylon would be like when he woke. She remembered how dark his mind had been when she'd entered it. She didn't want to think about what that darkness would look like in conscious form.

Pushing her thoughts aside, Brijit watched as the Elder healer began running her hands over Weylon's forehead and chanting in the ancient Elder language. Although she wasn't completely fluent in the language, Brijit didn't recognize the dialect Nestariel was using.

At first nothing seemed to be happening, and then Brijit saw Weylon's fingers begin to twitch ever so slightly. After a few moments a low groan escaped from him.

"Weylon, can you hear me?" Brijit moved to the side of the bed and took his hand instinctively.

Nestariel stopped her chanting and looked a Brijit with raised eyebrows. Her gaze dropped to where Brijit's fingers were laced with Weylon's. Understanding dawned in her eyes, and she shook her head in disappointment at Brijit. Apparently Nestariel was more perceptive than Brijit had given her credit for.

But Brijit ignored her and focused instead on Weylon, who was opening his eyes.

"Brijit?" His voice was raspy and weak from disuse.

She nodded. "I'm here."

He gave a weak smile. "Don't look so worried. I'm okay."

"Weylon, you were attacked. What do you remember?"

He looked around his surroundings. When his gaze fell on Nestariel, he struggled to sit up, but Brijit put her hand on his chest and gently pushed down, hoping to reassure him. He looked around the room franticly. "Where are we?"

"We are safe for now. We are with the Elders," Brijit soothed.

Weylon only looked more panicked. Nestariel spoke then.

"I am Nestariel. You are at Tèarmann, my home. And you are safe for as long as you are within the walls and do no one here harm."

Brijit looked at Nestariel in surprise. "Why do you think he might hurt anyone?" she asked in confusion.

Nestariel did not answer. Instead she turned to Brijit. "Now that you've seen he is well you need to rest yourself. I will escort you to your chambers."

Brijit opened her mouth to protest. She wanted to make sure Weylon was quite well. And she wanted to talk to him about what happened. But before she could say a word, Nestariel cut her off.

"You came here for a purpose, Brijit, and that purpose was not to care for your fellow *Coimirceoirí*." Her voice was steely and tinged with a hint of warning. "I am the healer in this dwelling, and I will take care of him."

"It's okay, Brijit," Weylon said weakly. "Nestariel is right. You look exhausted. Get some rest and I will see you soon." He squeezed her fingers tightly. She felt a gentle prodding at her mind, but Brijit kept her shield in place, ignoring the look of hurt on Weylon's face. She wasn't ready to open her mind to Weylon just yet, not after what had happened in the forest. She didn't yet want to know if his mind was free or not. At the moment she just wanted to keep those dark voices at bay.

"Weylon needs sleep as well," Nestariel said. Brijit knew the Elder was right.

"Okay. I will check on you tomorrow," she told him.

The hurt disappeared. She hoped he just thought she was tired.

He smiled faintly and then closed his eyes again.

Brijit gave his fingers a final squeeze before she turned and followed Nestariel out of the room.

They had not gone more than a few feet from the closed door to Weylon's room when Nestariel turned to her in anger. "How could you have become intimate with a *Coimirceoirí*? You know the rules. You are bound to the Elders and forbidden to have relations."

Brijit stepped back as if the woman had struck her.

"We are not intimate," she denied in horror.

Nestariel shook her head. “Perhaps not physically but you have bonded emotionally, and I don’t mean in the way that is common for *Coimirceoirí*.” The old woman glared at her. “You stupid, stupid girl!”

Brijit bristled at that. “Another Elder rule meant to control *Coimirceoirí*?” she asked bitterly.

Nestariel paused and then laughed. “Is that what you think? That these rules exist for your punishment?”

Brijit flushed at the mocking tone in the Elder’s voice.

“Listen, my child, the last time two chosen *Coimirceoirí* bonded, two who only had a fraction of the gifts you and that boy have, the safety of both Séreméla and the entire Five Corners was threatened.”

Brijit’s heart dropped. “Who were they?” she whispered even though she already knew the answer.

“Ester and Kale.”

When Nestariel saw the horror on Brijit’s face, she gentled her tone. “I see they do teach you some things at that decrepit old Academy, anyway.” Suddenly she looked up and down the hallway and said in a hushed tone, “We will speak more in your room.”

With that she began striding quickly down the hallway. The passage ended in a stairwell, which Nestariel started to climb. Three stories, later she led Brijit down another hallway and then finally stopped outside a door.

She opened it and beckoned to her. Inside was a large bed that immediately grabbed Brijit’s attention. In the corner was a porcelain washing tub that had been filled recently with steaming water. Brijit longed to soak the grime of the journey off her and then fall into the bed.

Nestariel seemed to read her mind. “You may soak while we talk,” she said.

Brijit hesitated, not wanting to disrobe in front of this ancient Elder whom she’d just met.

Nestariel just stood there looking at her. "Don't be bashful. I've seen more bodies than you can imagine. Your water is getting cold."

Brijit glanced at the tub and saw rose petals floating on the surface. Throwing caution to the wind, she pulled off her grimy clothes and sunk into the warm water with a sigh of contentment.

"Now, let us talk about what you have done," Nestariel said.

Brijit's opened her eyes and looked at the old woman. Stupid, stupid, stupid! The Elder now had her trapped in the water and could interrogate as much as she wished.

"I've done nothing wrong," Brijit insisted.

"Haven't you? The fact that you can't see what you've done should be enough proof that you have no idea what you are getting into."

Brijit stared at the old woman in confusion.

"What do you mean what I'm getting into?"

Nestariel sat down on the edge of the bed and ran her hand over her face. She looked old and tired. It was disconcerting to see an Elder like Nestariel. Brijit was so accustomed to seeing Elders who were youthful and flawless. She wondered why Nestariel was different.

Brijit sunk deeper in her tub, willing the warm water to chase away the chill that suddenly gripped her.

"I'm sorry, Brijit, but the *Coimirceoirí* have always been pawns of the Elders. You have been brought here for a specific purpose." She paused. "And your friend for another one. If the Elders know that you have feelings for one another, they will do everything they can to punish you. Normally they would simply separate you, but things are more complicated than that. Your fates are tied up together, and with the plans they have for you…" She shook her snowy head. "I can't explain it all to you tonight. Things were complicated enough before you started a relationship with Weylon, but they are more convoluted now."

Weylon and her hardly had a relationship and certainly not in the way that Nestariel was suggesting. But…Brijit paused for a moment.

"What makes it more convoluted?" Brijit asked.

"Weylon should have died in Jirgen Forest. No one, not even an Elder, survives an attack from the *Aptrgangr*."

Brijit stared at Nestariel, the earlier horror she'd felt beginning to build in her chest again.

The old woman took a deep breath and then continued. "No one knows precisely what the *Aptrgangr* are, but they have somehow emerged from The Rift, itself a place of great evil. Once an *Aptrgangr* has feasted on a creature, man or beast, there is no hope for survival. So what your grandmother told you is sacred information."

She paused and stared out the window at the gathering dusk. "Do you know how your grandmother came to know of these mushrooms that you gave Weylon?"

Brijit shook her head. She had no idea how her grandmother had known of such things. She hadn't questioned it at the time. After all, her grandmother had always been a great healer. "I assumed she got it from one of her books or scrolls."

Nestariel's eyes turned to Brijit and sharpened with interest. "Your grandmother had scrolls?"

Brijit nodded. "She had a great library that took up far too much of her small dwelling. She insisted on keeping everything, though. She said each one contained precious information."

"A mere village healer had such a complete library?" Nestariel began muttering to herself. Slowly her eyes focused on Brijit again. "Never mind, it will have to wait for another time."

Brijit didn't ask what the old woman was muttering about. Instead, she asked what had been bothering her most. "Why was saving Weylon so bad?" she asked quietly.

Now Nestariel's expression turned to one of sympathy.

"Because my child, you couldn't save him. He was already gone. All you did was prolong the inevitable. The poison that is left in his system will slowly, over time, eat away at the Weylon you know until nothing good is left."

Brijit shook her head, refusing to believe it. Weylon had seemed just like himself when he woke.

"It could take decades for the full extent of the damage to be complete," Nestariel explained. "I'm sorry, child. I know it would have been difficult to see someone you love die in your arms in such a way. But now you must watch him be eaten slowly from within. And that will be infinitely worse."

Brijit looked down at the now-wilted rose petals sinking to the bottom of her bath. She remembered the red eyes and matted fur of the creature that had attacked Weylon. Had she condemned him to one day evolve into something like that beast? Suddenly Brijit wanted out of the tub.

Nestariel, as if reading her mind, handed her a warm towel and gestured toward a clean white nightgown, laid out on the foot of the bed.

"I suggest you get some rest while you can. Your work here is just about to begin." And with those last words the Elder turned and left the chamber.

Chapter Eleven

As soft and appealing as the bed was after weeks on the road, Brijit had a restless night spent tossing and turning. As much as she tried, she couldn't chase Nestariel's words from her mind. The idea that Weylon was somehow infected with the poison was difficult to accept. But she couldn't forget the voices that had whispered to her from Weylon's mind.

She remembered, too, her grandmother's warning. She had predicted that Weylon would be the end of Brijit. Her grandmother had told her that it was her fate. Brijit hadn't wanted to believe it, but now Nestariel had essentially said the same thing. Brijit couldn't help wondering if there could be some truth to her grandmother's warning?

When she'd finally fallen asleep it had been in the early morning hours, and it seemed like just moments after she'd settled before a knock on her door woke her.

A young Elder girl of exquisite beauty opened the door and looked in at her with the friendliest smile she'd seen on the face of any Elder.

"Hello, Brijit! I'm Raina," she announced as she placed a tray of fruit next to the bed.

Brijit sat up, rubbing her eyes.

"Oh, you still look so tired," Raina said with sympathy. "I'm so sorry but I have to wake you and get you ready."

"Ready?" Brijit asked.

The girl nodded. "For your meeting with Princess Neirdre."

Brijit snapped awake. She'd had no idea she was meeting with Princess Neirdre that morning.

She looked at Raina in alarm. The girl smiled sympathetically.

"Here, eat something, while I lay out some clean clothing for you," Raina said as she handed Brijit the plate of fruit.

Brijit watched as the girl crossed to the closet and pulled out a dress made of soft peach fabric and lay it on the foot of the bed.

"What is she like?" Brijit asked as she nibbled on a strawberry.

Raina paused and seemed to consider her answer for a few moments. Then she smiled.

"She is like a princess," she said cheerfully as if that explained everything.

Brijit frowned.

"Don't worry, you will do fine," Raina soothed when she saw Brijit's expression.

But that was the problem, wasn't it? She didn't know what she was supposed to do. She had no idea why she was here or meeting with Princess Neirdre and yet everyone was acting as if she should know exactly what was going on.

Raina held up the dress invitingly, and Brijit stood up. There was only one way to find out the reasons for her being here: she would have to meet the princess.

#

The princess of the Elders was a woman who possessed an ethereal beauty so perfect that tears pricked at Brijit's eyes when she saw her. Despite her great beauty, at first Princess Neirdre seemed to be kind and welcoming. Brijit sank into a curtsy, but Princess Neirdre took her hand and lifted her out of it almost immediately.

"I'm glad you are here, Brijit Carnesîr," she said as she clasped Brijit's clammy hand in hers. "I apologize for any distress the secrecy of your journey may have caused you. I know you had believed you were going to Séreméla. This is not at all what you expected, I'm sure."

Brijit kept her face clear of all emotion and her shield firmly in place, although she doubted the princess had the power to read someone's mind. She didn't want the Elders to know that she had known Sérémela was not their final destination. She wished she'd been able to speak with Weylon the previous evening.

"Come, sit and have some refreshments," Princess Neirdre said as she turned to a small table laid with tea and an assortment of baked treats. Brijit's stomach growled in spite of herself. She'd been too exhausted to eat the evening meal that had been sent to her the previous night, and this morning she hadn't had time to eat more than a few quick nibbles of the fruit Raina brought to her.

As Princess Neirdre sat, her hand went automatically to her rounded lower abdomen, an age-old sign that she was cradling a babe in her womb. Brijit smiled in spite of herself.

"You know why you were the student chosen this year?" Princess Neirdre asked as Brijit reached for a tiny, delicate cake. Brijit froze with the cake in her fingers and waited for the princess to speak again.

She smiled slightly, and Brijit noticed for the first time that the smile did not reach her eyes.

"We've been watching you since before you were first sent to the Academy, you know. Your skills as a healer and midwife were noted even in Sérémela." Her hand went to her stomach again. "It was always obvious that you would be coming to us. We just had to find the right male *Coimirceoirí* to accompany you."

Brijit was surprised. She thought Weylon was the one they had chosen from the start, but it appeared that the Elders had wanted her all along.

"We were fortunate that Weylon Forborrow was in the same year as you. He has proven exceptionally useful."

Princess Neirdre stared distastefully at the cake that was still suspended between Brijit's fingertips midway to her mouth. Horrified Brijit stuffed the tiny morsel into her mouth and dropped her eyes to her plate.

"The child is a girl. Our best healers have confirmed this. I'm sure you already suspected as much."

Brijit still didn't say anything. She was not gifted in guessing the gender of an unborn child. Her grandmother had always said it was impossible to tell for certain until a child was born. But she did wonder why the Elders had need of her when it was clear that their own healers had already assessed Princess Neirdre.

"Your value comes from the fact you are not Elder," Princess Neirdre said as if she had read her mind.

Brijit wondered what the motive could be in having a non-Elder healer as the princess's personal midwife? She remembered how brutal the female Elder had been when she killed the child in the cottage; how quickly it had happened. Did Princess Neirdre fear something similar could happen to her child? But surely the royalty would be guarded so that the child would be safe with or without the mark.

Before Brijit could think of a way to put the question running through her mind to the princess, an older Elder woman entered the room. She walked with a regal air and came and sat beside Princess Neirdre. At once Brijit was aware of the resemblance between the two.

"Brijit, this is my mother, Erulassë. She will be involved in all aspects of my confinement. Mother, Brijit is the *Coimirceoirí* who will care for us."

Erulassë raised her eyebrows as her gaze swept over Brijit and then seemed to dismiss her.

"Surely an Elder midwife would have sufficed, my daughter," Erulassë said coolly. "If not, then someone more," she paused and looked at Brijit again, "experienced as a midwife."

Brijit tried to keep her face clear so the Elder woman would not see how her words had stung. She knew many Elders thought the *Coimirceoirí* were unnecessary in modern times. They believed the *Coimirceoirí* were part of an old and dated tradition that took opportunities away from Elders themselves. Many modern-day Elders believed that they were more than capable of providing healers and guardians to the royal family, ones who were themselves Elders and thus understood their ways.

Erulassë was not likely to be the only Elder who felt this way. Brijit would have to become accustomed to such talk, especially when they went to Séreméla.

But for now she would have to find a way to work with Erulassë until her grandchild was born.

Princess Neirdre scowled at her mother. "This is the one chosen. You know that. Why are you always difficult?"

Erulassë merely shrugged and reached for a tiny berry tart on the tray. She nibbled it for a moment before putting it down on a small plate and standing.

"As always, you will do as you think best, my daughter." And with those parting words, Erulassë swept from the room as regal as when she had entered.

Princess Neirdre glared after her mother's form with narrowed eyes. "She is always trying to dictate how I live and the choices I make. She forgets too often that I am the Crown Prince's bride.

Brijit smiled in what she hoped was understanding. "I'm sure to her you will always be her little girl."

Princess Neirdre snorted in an unroyal manner.

"I was never her 'little girl.' The wet nurse cared for me until my governess took over."

Brijit could hear the pain in her voice, but the princess seemed to be unaware of it. Brijit was surprised. She had assumed the Neirdre and her mother were close since the princess had insisted that she was to be so involved in Neirdre's pregnancy. Brijit said as much to the princess.

Neirdre laughed, "Oh, no! She hates all this. I don't think she was even conscious for my birth. I'm making her take part because she despised it so much."

Brijit tried to hide her shock. She couldn't imagine being so cruel toward one's parent. Her own parents had been killed when she was small and her grandmother had raised her. But even with Grandmamma's sometimes eccentric views, Brijit would never have dreamed of speaking against her.

Neirdre was glaring at the door through which Erulassë had disappeared. After a moment, she turned her attention back to Brijit.

"You have met the sorceress, I assume?"

Brijit started. Sorceress?

At her confused look, the princess laughed. "Of course, Nestariel would not have introduced herself as such. She never does. She prefers to use terms like 'healer' or 'prophet.'" Princess Neirdre narrowed her eyes. "I suspect she would use 'healer' with you."

Brijit nodded.

"Well, she is a healer but not one I would allow to touch either my daughter or myself. She delves in magik. Of course, living this close to The Rift, you can hardly blame her."

Neirdre didn't seem to care what Brijit's response might be. She continued speaking, "Did she tell you that this is her refuge?"

Brijit nodded noncommittally. Nestariel *had* told her that this was her home. Brijit had just assumed that she was employed by the Elder royals, she hadn't realized that Nestariel was the actual mistress of the fortress.

Princess Neirdre stood and strode over to the huge window that took up part of the western wall. "I don't know why she would want to live here. But it is what she chose a long time ago." She turned back to Brijit. "She is my aunt, of course. My mother's sister."

Brijit was further stunned by this news. Nestariel bore little resemblance to Erulassë. She seemed decades older than the princess's mother.

"Living here has aged her prematurely," Princess Neirdre explained offhandedly as she anticipated Brijit's question.

Or living in Séreméla had kept the princess's mother youthful, Brijit thought to herself. She had heard many rumors about the magik that was used to keep Séreméla the paradise the Elders coveted. But she wouldn't say such a thing to the woman in front of her.

"She talks in riddles always," the princess went on, her tone almost whiney. "She never says anything clearly and then when you question her she slips into the ancient language and only that old friend of hers speaks that dialect. She thinks we should all keep the old language alive. It's ridiculous."

"Friend?" Brijit asked.

"Former lover, if you believe the rumors. I don't know. They are so ancient that the thought of either of them having a lover makes me ill. His name is Eöl Ar-Feiniel. You probably will meet him. He followed my husband here. Why the Crown Prince has need of the old man, I do not know."

Princess Neirdre came back to her chair and lowered herself gracefully. "We wouldn't have come here except we had to, you know. As soon as they told us it was a girl, we knew we had to flee. There were too many on the council who would just as soon kill me and her as risk having a new queen." She sighed. "I hate it here. You can almost feel the evil. But my husband said it was the only place our enemies wouldn't dare to come. I just hope that we can return to Séreméla after Minathrial is born."

Brijit raised her eyebrows. "Minathrial?" she asked.

"Oh, yes, her name has been chosen for generations. The next queen of the Elders."

Brijit smiled and nodded politely. But to herself she thought how strange it must be to not be able to choose your own child's name.

"I just hope she comes soon. I long to return home."

She smiled at Brijit and suddenly Brijit's breath was taken away once again by the sheer beauty in front of her. "I'm so glad you are here, Brijit Carnesîr. You have been foretold to do great things. And you will be a wonderful chaperone for my daughter." Her hand went to her swollen stomach again. "She is the future of our people. We must all keep her safe."

Chapter Twelve

Brijit had taken to visiting Nestariel in her rooms when she wasn't busy with the princess. As Tèarmann was Nestariel's home, it wasn't unexpected that the old Elder had an entire wing of the fortress as her private quarters. What Brijit was surprised to find was that the wing was filled primarily with books.

On her first visit to Nestariel's rooms, Brijit met Eöl Ar-Feiniel, of whom the princess had spoken of so negatively. The old Elder was the only one Brijit had seen who actually looked older than Nestariel.

"Hello, *Coimirceoirí*, I have already heard much about you from Nestariel," he said as he took her hand on their first meeting.

"You have?" Brijit was surprised.

"Yes. You are a unique and very talented girl, I hear. What you did in Jirgen Forest is extraordinary."

Brijit was stunned. This was the first time anyone had suggested that what she had done to save Weylon was not a negative thing.

"Eöl Ar-Feiniel thrives on experiments and puzzle solving, my dear," Nestariel told her wryly. "He finds the mix of *Kurunii* and *Coimirceoirí* intriguing."

The old man ignored her. "Of course, it's intriguing. Why no one else took an interest in this or prepared her properly is beyond me."

"Well, I agree with you there," Nestariel murmured and then changed the topic. "So, my dear, how did you find my lovely niece?"

Brijit hesitated before answering.

"You can be honest, my dear. I personally think she's a spoiled brat."

Brijit hid a smile. "Well, she does seem to have a mind of her own," she said diplomatically. "But she's excited about her baby."

Nestariel's eyes narrowed. "You mean she's excited to give birth to the next queen of the Elders." The old Elder sighed. "Sadly, my niece is not at all excited about actually becoming a mother. Her husband seems more eager for the child to arrive."

Brijit privately agreed with Nestariel. Princess Neirdre's fixation on having a girl-child was disconcerting. But feeling uncomfortable speaking ill of the princess who she was *Coimirceoirí* for, Brijit shifted her attention back to Eöl Ar-Feiniel.

"What are you doing?" she asked the old man.

He had multiple pieces of old parchment spread out in front of him and was scratching rapidly with a quill on another piece of parchment at his side.

He looked over at Brijit and smiled. "I'm translating the Prophecy, my dear."

Brijit's stomach dropped. The Prophecy.

The old man laughed when he saw her face. "Oh I know, the sacred text of the Elders and all that. Really it is just a bunch of pieces of paper that need to be deciphered."

Brijit smiled slightly, not sure she believed him.

"And how are you making out with that?" she asked.

"It's slow and tedious work," Nestariel answered for him. "But he loves it."

Nestariel's eyes warmed as they rested on the man sitting across from her. Brijit's heart pinched when she saw the love in her eyes. Eöl Ar-Feiniel clearly meant a lot to Nestariel.

Later, when Brijit left Nestariel's rooms, the old woman followed her into the halls. She looked strained now she was out of Eöl Ar-Feiniel's presence.

"I know you've been wanting to see Weylon, Brijit. He is doing much better, and I think he would be up for a short visit now."

For a reason she couldn't explain, Brijit hesitated. She missed Weylon, and it was true that she wanted to talk to him, but an image of him being consumed by evil suddenly filled her mind. She recoiled from it and shook her head. "I don't think I'm ready to see him," she admitted softly.

Nestariel's face tightened. "But you've been asking almost constantly to see him."

"I know," Brijit admitted, feeling ashamed of herself. She just wasn't ready to see what she had done to Weylon yet. What if he wasn't the same boy she'd come to care for so strongly? What if she had destroyed him?

Nestariel narrowed her eyes. "Getting this first meeting over with will help both of you on the road to healing."

She was probably right, but Brijit still could not bring herself to do it. Instead she nodded and murmured, "I will soon."

Nestariel watched her for a moment until Brijit started to feel uncomfortable. To shift the Elder's attention off of her, she changed the subject. "Eöl Ar-Feiniel seems nice."

Nestariel laughed. "Subtle, my dear," but her face softened as she looked back over her shoulder. "He is one of the most gifted archivists that we have ever had."

"Do you think he will translate the Prophecy?"

Nestariel turned back to her and shook her head slightly. "The Prophecy can't be translated in just one lifetime, my dear, not even in the long lifetime of an Elder. It will take generations before we know the secrets that lie in that document."

Those words were still ringing in Brijit's head as she headed back to her room. The Prophecy it seemed was not translatable, despite what so many now believed.

#

Weylon wandered through the fortress wondering where Brijit was. He had only seen her once since he'd woken up and that visit had been supervised by Nestariel, the strange Elder healer who continually looked at him with suspicion through her eerily dark-green eyes. He knew she didn't trust him, but he didn't understand why.

And she seemed to wholly disapprove of his relationship with Brijit. It was obvious from the way she looked at the two of them that she thought they were more than just friends. Regardless of what he might feel for Brijit, the truth was they hadn't taken their relationship further than friendship. Not that Nestariel would believe him. He could tell the old Elder had already made up her mind on the matter.

Weylon knew that it was against Elder tradition to let *Coimirceoirí* become romantically involved, but there seemed to be more than just disapproval of their relationship in Nestariel's expression. It was almost as if she were guarding Brijit from him. It was ridiculous. He was the last person Brijit needed protection from. The truth was Weylon would do anything to make sure she was safe.

While he understood that they were in Nestariel's fortress, he didn't know what the Elders' plans were for him. Apparently Brijit had already been briefed on the reason for her being here. She had been chosen to help Princess Neirdre bring her child into the world safely. Why an Elder midwife had not been chosen, Weylon did not know.

In the meantime, he'd had no luck in discerning why the Elders had brought him to Tèarmann. He had asked Nestariel about it each time she came to tend to his dressing but she had given him no clear answers. She had merely said that he needed to rest and recover from his injuries and that his purpose would be revealed in time.

Weylon was irritated with this secrecy. He already felt wholly recovered from the injury. In fact, the bandage that still covered his wound had remained clean and dry for the last two days. It was clear he didn't need it anymore, and yet Nestariel kept changing it once a day and encouraging him to rest. He didn't feel like resting; he felt like getting out.

So this morning that was exactly what he'd done. He had left his room and wandered through the fortress. He was mildly surprised that no one tried to stop him, but then again he was a guest here not a prisoner.

The fortress turned out to be much larger than he had anticipated. Of course, he had been unconscious when they arrived so he'd not had anything to gauge his assumptions about the place on. But as he wandered idly through the halls, he realized that it was as vast as a palace.

There was no way he would ever find Brijit in such a huge building. He would have to wait for her to come to him. But that didn't mean he couldn't explore.

An hour later he found himself on the ramparts at the top of the fortress looking westward. What he saw intrigued him. What could only be The Rift lay in the distance.

Weylon stared in fascination. So this was the legendary source of evil that threatened all of Five Corners. Part of him had always believed that it couldn't be real, that it must be a story made up to entertain the young *Coimirceoirí* students at Stone Mountain. But there was nothing imaginary about what lay to the west, right in front of him.

The Rift was far in the distance. As the desert approached it, the sand turned from pale brown to dark ebony. In fact, everything went black as it approached The Rift, as if that part of the earth was swallowing all light. Weylon looked into the distance and saw swirling darkness. It looked almost…alive.

A sudden eagerness he didn't understand rose up in his chest. It was like…he paused in his thoughts as he realized what he felt was excitement.

Slightly troubled that The Rift would elicit such an emotion from him, Weylon stepped back from the edge of the rampart.

"They say that looking into The Rift is suicidal."

He whirled and saw Nestariel watching him a few feet away. Her gaze was on him, but a shadow fell across her face so he couldn't clearly read her expression. "What do you feel when you look at it, I wonder, Weylon Forborrow?"

He blinked and stepped toward her. He didn't want to admit the keenness he'd felt in his breast.

"I feel nothing," he lied smoothly.

Nestariel smiled at him knowingly. "And so it begins."

Weylon watched her in confusion. But she didn't elaborate on her words. Instead she said what he'd been waiting to hear.

"You are wanted. The Crown Prince has requested an audience."

#

Suiadan, the reigning Crown Prince of the Elders was waiting for Weylon in the training ground. Weylon was surprised to see the Elder knights running through training exercises very similar to what he and the other *Coimirceoirí* students had done at Stone Mountain. The prince, himself, was not partaking in the training but observing it.

Weylon came before him and, not knowing what was expected, bowed slightly in deference.

Suiadan laughed. "You don't need to rely on pleasantries. This is not what I would call a civilized place, Weylon Forborrow."

Weylon raised his head and nodded. He liked this Crown Prince already.

"Come, we will walk." Suiadan led him away from the training grounds and Weylon noted that three Elder guards trailed them. The Crown Prince either didn't feel safe in Weylon's presence or he didn't feel safe at Tèarmann. Either way, Weylon respected him for taking precautions. A man in his position could never be too safe.

"You are probably wondering what your task will be, *Coimirceoirí*," the Crown Prince said wryly. "Particularly when you know that we handpicked you from the rest of your year because of your fighting ability. But as you can see, I am well protected and I have a large group of warriors with me. So why would I want a male *Coimirceoirí* apprentice of your skill set?"

Suiadan was correct. Weylon had wondered about that, but he kept silent, waiting for the Crown Prince to continue.

"Your job is not to protect me. In fact, your job may not be fully revealed for years hence." He paused as they approached the rampart Weylon had stood on earlier with Nestariel. Together they stood and looked out to The Rift. Once again Weylon felt a stirring deep in his chest as he gazed upon the swirling darkness in the distance. Unbidden excitement flared to life. Suiadan did not gaze into the darkness. Instead he studied Weylon.

"But a complication has arisen with you, *Coimirceoirí*. And the decision rests with me to determine your fate."

Weylon looked at him in surprise. He knew of no complication that had changed his mission or his loyalty to the Elders. He looked back at the darkness in the distance.

"I have been told that you have been bitten by the *Aptrgangr* and yet you stand before me. You do realize that should not be possible."

Weylon forced his gaze away from The Rift once more and looked at the Crown Prince beside him in confusion.

"Oh, you didn't know of this." A look of understanding dawned on Suiadan's face. "A creature from The Rift is deadly to all mortals." The prince paused and studied Weylon for a long moment. "And yet you are still alive. Or so it would seem."

Weylon shook his head. "Are you suggesting I am dead?" His tone was terse.

The prince held his gaze for a long moment. "Not precisely. But you are not what you were before the attack, either. I think you know this, Weylon Forborrow."

Weylon wondered if the Crown Prince of the Elders was crazed in his mind. What he said made no sense.

"You think I'm out of mind, and yet you are too smart to say so." Suiadan laughed. "I like that." He clapped Weylon on the shoulder but then his expression became somber.

"You will understand, *Coimirceoirí*, that this is a vulnerable time for my family. My wife carries a girl-child in her womb."

Weylon sucked in his breath. A new ruler for the Elders. A true ruler for the first time in twelve generations.

"Yes, I see you know what that means. That is why we find ourselves in such an unpalatable place." The prince looked out to the swirling darkness. "My wife is less than thrilled with our current living arrangements, but it is necessary to ensure the safe delivery of my daughter."

Weylon could understand that.

"After she is born, however, the real work will begin. And that is where you will come in." Suiadan paused. "Or at least that was the original plan. Now I'm not so sure it would be wise to entrust you with my daughter's safety."

Weylon opened his mouth to protest. He had pledged allegiance to the Elders. That wasn't about to change.

But Suiadan held up his hand anticipating his protests and silencing him. "Your heart is strong, which is why your woman was able to bring you back from sure death. But what she has done is not natural."

Weylon tried to ignore the fact that even the Crown Prince seemed to think that Brijit was his mate. Instead, he focused on the rest of Suiadan's words.

"What do you mean?" Weylon asked bluntly.

"The poison from the *Aptrgangr* is still within you, Weylon. It is not strong enough to kill you or even affect you negatively for some time. Years, decades even."

Weylon shook his head. He felt fine. In fact, he felt better than fine.

Suiadan watched him closely. "You feel good since you've recovered?" he asked, knowingly.

Weylon nodded.

"Better than good, in fact?"

Warily, Weylon nodded again.

"I'll be willing to wager that you have never felt so alive."

Weylon stepped away from the Crown Prince, feeling his throat closing just a little.

"You will continue to feel this alive for a very long time. But eventually the poison will ravage your brain, and you will not be yourself anymore." The prince paused. "Your healer girl saved you only to destroy you."

Weylon shook his head. Brijit would never do such a thing.

"She didn't know what she was doing," Suiadan told him, easily reading his thoughts. "She thought she was saving you. She is pure of heart and couldn't have harmed you even if she tried. But what she has done remains for you to accept and learn to live with."

Weylon swallowed, not wanting to believe what the Elder prince was telling him, but a sinking feeling deep inside told him that Suiadan had no reason to lie to him.

"You should also know that just any *Coimirceoirí* healer could not have done this. Only a *Kurunii* who uses magik could have saved you." He paused, musing. "Or a *Draíodóir*, I suppose, but they are all male and your savior was decidedly female."

Weylon stared at Suiadan in horror. He was saying Brijit was a practitioner of witchcraft.

"You will have to deal with what this means for you and Brijit as you move forward. But I have to consider larger things." The prince paused. "Having you on my side could be useful."

Weylon narrowed his eyes, wondering what the prince was getting at.

"I have no doubt that you will be loyal to the royal family for a very long time, Weylon Forborrow. And given your considerable skill set, I would be foolish not to use you," he continued as if he were thinking aloud. In fact, it appeared that he had forgotten Weylon was even there. "Still the risk is high. My advisors have told me that it is not worth the risk. That I should have my guards kill you immediately. But I have chosen to ignore them for the present."

Weylon's chest loosened in relief. He had trained to be the royal family's chosen *Coimirceoirí* for too long to have it all snuffed out before it even started. He was determined not to give the Crown Prince any reason to dismiss him from his position.

"You will be the protector of my daughter, Minathrial, her guardian until you are no long able to do so."

Weylon was surprised. Elder tradition was such that a *Coimirceoir* would be assigned to any living princess. A *Coimirceoir* was different than the *Coimirceoirí* in that it was always a male Elder who was assigned to the heir of the throne upon her birth. Generally, one did not need both *Coimirceoirí* and a *Coimirceoir.*

It had been centuries since the Elders had had a queen on their throne, but Weylon did not think they would forget the role of the *Coimirceoir*. Suiadan's next words answered his thoughts.

"She will, of course, be assigned a *Coimirceoir*; however, he is a boy of only one year right now. Until he is able to take up his duty, she will need you."

The prince turned suddenly from the ramparts.

"There will be those who think I've lost my mind for trusting you, but something tells me that there is a reason you have made it this far, Weylon Forborrow. And that is good enough for me."

Chapter Thirteen

Brijit knew she had to stop avoiding Weylon. It was true that she had been busy with Princess Neirdre, who was demanding in the extreme. But she was not so busy that she couldn't see him at all. The truth was, Brijit was scared to see Weylon. She didn't want to see what she had done to him.

Her nights had become plagued with dreams of Weylon. They started sweetly enough, but throughout the dream he would morph into a hideous extension of the creature that had attacked him in the dead forest. They always ended the same, his blackened body pierced by a hundred Elder arrows and his face turning to her ask, "Why did you do this to me? Why?"

Nestariel seemed to sense Brijit's unease. The Elder urged her to see Weylon.

"What is done is done. I was angry with you in the beginning, but he is still more the man you know than anything else. You have to understand that the poison that is in his system will take a very long time to affect him." Nestariel brushed a stray hair off Brijit's forehead in a gesture so gentle it brought tears to Brijit's eyes, before adding, "And I have need of Weylon's company on a trip you and I will be taking. It would be better if you had talked to him before then."

Brijit looked up in surprise. She hadn't expected to leave the fortress before the birth of Princess Neirdre's daughter. And her stomach dropped as she thought of spending all that time with Weylon.

"I'm not sure it's wise to leave Princess Neirdre."

"It is a short trip. We will be gone two days only, and the child will not come until the next moon at least."

Brijit raised her eyebrows at this but Nestariel just laughed at her.

"You have birthed many children for one so young, but I have seen thousands of souls into this world. We will be back long before she will be born."

Brijit knew arguing more with Nestariel was pointless. Resigned, she turned to go pack her things for the trip. But Nestariel's next words had her stopping in her tracks.

"We are going to your grandmother's home."

Pain stabbed through her, and Brijit recoiled in shock. Her grandmother's home? Why?

"I have need of what lies there," Nestariel explained. And Brijit remembered the Elder's keen interest when she's mentioned her grandmother's scrolls and books.

"I also think you would be more at ease if you knew whether or not your grandmother was alive."

Brijit hesitated and then nodded. It was true. As much as she wanted to forget what had happened in her vision, she needed to know if Nestariel was correct in assuming that her grandmother was dead. In fact, she needed to know what exactly had happened to Grandmamma.

"When do we leave?"

#

Nestariel wasted no time in starting the journey to Brijit's grandmother's home. To Brijit's surprise, Princess Neirdre, who had been demanding of late, didn't protest.

"I must leave for a few days," Brijit told her nervously, expecting Princess Neirdre to explode with outrage.

But she merely waved her hand in front of her face as she lounged with a book in her lap. "Go. She will not come before you return."

She had taken to talking of her unborn child as if she knew everything there was to know about her baby. But Brijit wasn't so certain that Princess Neirdre was as in touch with the infant as she wanted everyone to believe. She seemed more focused on what she was missing back in Séreméla than what was going on with her child. Neirdre never missed the chance to whine about the parties and events that were happening in her homeland without her. And the fact that she was forbidden to communicate with her friends in Séreméla only made her more self-pitying. But the Crown Prince had been adamant that they keep their location a secret. He had insisted upon it as a precaution for protecting their unborn child. Neirdre was smart enough to agree with her husband on that front.

Brijit stood in the doorway, watching the lounging princess for a few moments longer, wondering what kind of mother she would be and if she would even have to be a mother, given that she had others to fend for her every need. It seemed that Neirdre did very little of anything. She would read books about Elder fashion and simple history volumes about former princesses as if she were making sure that she was playing the role correctly. But as far as Brijit could tell, there wasn't much she did beyond that.

Neirdre had not been royal by birth but had acquired her title through her husband. Although the way both she and her mother paraded around, one would think that she came from a royal line. From what Brijit understood, Neirdre and her mother were from a family of Elders who had strong ties with the council and were often in the company of Elder royalty. It had been decided from an early age that she would be suitable wife to the Crown Prince. But she showed little love or concern for her husband. She just acted as if their lives had unfolded the way they were meant to.

Brijit thought it was sad. She wasn't so naïve as to believe that all marriages, particularly royal marriages, were based on love; however, the relationship between Neirdre and the Crown Prince seemed to be nothing more than a business deal. Neirdre was enjoying her end of the bargain and Brijit supposed the Crown Prince got his heirs from the deal. It still seemed like a sad arrangement to Brijit.

As Brijit left Neirdre's chamber she wondered what the princess would do if the child she carried turned out to not be the girl-child the Elder healers had predicted. Brijit had no concrete reason to think this might be so, but she'd been having disturbing dreams of late.

As she made her way to the meeting point that Nestariel had arranged, Brijit was preoccupied by thoughts of a dream she'd had the previous night. In it Princess Neirdre had indeed given birth but not to the girl everyone was expecting. Instead she gave birth to a son. The royals were in an uproar about it, Neirdre most of all.

When Brijit awoke, she couldn't shake the feeling that there was some truth in the dream vision. But Princess Neirdre had told her that the Elders' most trusted wise people had predicted the birth of a girl. It didn't make any sense. Surely the Elder healers knew more than any one. There was no reason for them to lie, was there?

Both Nestariel and Weylon were waiting in the stable when Brijit arrived. Thoughts of Princess Neirdre and her unborn child soon fled. She had her own problems to deal with. Foremost was Weylon.

Brijit felt guilty for having avoided him during his recovery. And now that she saw the hurt expression in his brown eyes, she felt a sharp prick of shame. He had done nothing to deserve this from her. Regardless of what the attack had done to him, it was not his fault. He had been innocent. He hadn't even had a choice when she had healed him – that had been her own doing.

And that was more than half the problem. Guilt threatened to consume Brijit when she thought of Weylon. She had wanted to save him for selfish reasons: she couldn't bear to lose him. The irony was that now she had ensured he would live she was scared to see what the poison would do to him.

Weylon moved to help her mount, but Brijit avoided his touch and instead pulled herself easily into her saddle. Fresh hurt flashed through his brown eyes, but Brijit pretended not to see it. She saw Nestariel press her lips together as she observed their interaction and was thankful when the old woman said nothing. As they left the fortress, Weylon brought his horse astride her own.

"I haven't seen you in a few weeks, Brijit."

She acknowledged his comment with a tilting of her head.

"Have you been ill?"

Brijit was surprised. She hadn't considered that he might be worried about her. She looked at him then. He looked so healthy, even more fit than during their journey. Her heart squeezed and she realized she was happy to see him. She had missed him.

"I've been fine," she answered. "Just busy with Princess Neirdre."

He nodded thoughtfully. "I've heard that she is quite demanding."

Why did he have to be so understanding? Surely he must know that she had been avoiding him. Brijit felt another stab of shame.

Turning to him she said, "How have you being keeping? Nestariel tells me you have recovered."

"Yes, I was going mad being confined to bed when it wasn't necessary."

Brijit smiled. "I can imagine." She couldn't picture Weylon being kept in a bed for too long. He was far too active for that. Brijit relaxed a bit, but his next words had her tensing again.

"Listen, Brijit, we need to talk about what happened in Jirgen Forest."

Brijit stared straight ahead. She knew he was right, but she didn't really want to talk about it. Especially not now as they were heading out on this journey.

"Do you really think this is the best time?"

Weylon's calm exterior finally cracked a bit. "Perhaps not, but when is the best time? I've been trying to talk to you, but you've been avoiding me like the plague."

Brijit did not try to deny it. She had been avoiding him. But if there was any hope that Nestariel was wrong, that Grandmamma was still alive, then perhaps her grandmother could help explain what she had done to Weylon and how she had saved him.

She pulled her mount closer to his horse and reached over, placing her hand on his strong forearm. She squeezed. His eyes met her own.

"Please, can we talk about it once we get to my grandmother's house? I just…" she looked ahead to where Nestariel was riding. "I promise I will tell you what happened there."

Weylon nodded and watched her face for a moment longer before looking ahead to the road. Brijit removed her hand.

Then he smiled suddenly. "Don't worry. I'm not mad at you. I just want to remember what happened. I only have fragments of memories, and I don't know what is real and what isn't." He looked back at her and Brijit was surprised to see the warmth in his brown eyes. "I owe you my life, Brijit. I will always be grateful for that."

Her heart twisted, and as she looked down, guilt stabbed at her. Weylon had no idea the type of life she had consigned him to. And she wasn't so sure he would be grateful when he found out precisely what she had done.

Before she could dwell too long on her dark thoughts, he went on, "To be honest I don't feel any different than I did before the attack. If anything, I feel more alive. But the Elders keep telling me that there is poison within me. That it's impossible to eradicate it all." He stopped talking for a moment. "The thing is, I don't feel worse. In fact, I feel *better* than I ever have in my life. The world seems more vibrant. The air is fresher; the food is tastier…you're prettier."

She looked at him quickly, heat filling her cheeks.

"Especially when you blush," he added with a grin, his tone teasing.

Brijit looked ahead again, not knowing how to reply. She didn't think Weylon would be so understanding when he learned the extent of what she had done to save him. She wondered just how much the Elders *had* told Weylon about what she'd done. She was sure it had only been the bare bones. There was no way he would be so understanding if he knew she had used magik to cure him. His next words surprised her.

"I've been thinking about it more and more, and I can't help wondering if they are wrong, Brijit." He lowered his voice even though Nestariel was well behind them. "What if the Elders have made a mistake this time? They can't possibly know everything that is going on. What if what you did actually cure me? It sure seems like that is what happened. I don't feel like I'm poisoned."

Hope filled Brijit's heart. Could it be possible that Weylon actually was better? She looked at him closely. He did look impossibly healthy and happy. His hair shone, his skin glowed and he exuded energy.

"Do you think that's possible?" she asked, her voice breathless.

He shrugged. "Isn't anything possible? They don't know everything, Brijit, despite what they would have the *Coimirceoirí* believe." His tone had taken on a bitter edge.

Brijit thought about that for a moment. He was right. The Elders couldn't know everything. She thought of Princess Neirdre and her insistence that she was giving birth to a girl-child even though Brijit's dreams told her otherwise. If the Elders were wrong about that, it was possible that they were wrong about Weylon as well.

"Brijit, I have seen no sign that I'm still infected with whatever poison that monster carried with it. You cured me. I'm certain of it." Weylon's tone was confident and sure.

A bit of the weight fell from Brijit's shoulders, and she smiled faintly at Weylon. If he felt that he was free of the evil, wasn't that the clearest sign that he actually was getting better? Surely he would know if he was still touched by the darkness; he would feel it inside him, slowly growing. And if they were wrong about that then maybe Nestariel was wrong about her grandmother being dead. Hope sprang to life in her chest. If Grandmamma was fine, then it could be possible that the Elders and all their beliefs were just superstition that had no basis in truth. Weylon was right: the Elders didn't know everything. And this time Brijit was sure they must have got it wrong.

#

Brijit's hopes were dashed as soon as she saw her grandmother's home, sitting dark and cold. A heavy foreboding filled her chest as as they approached the lifeless building that was once her home.

Although she hadn't been home more than five years, tears filled her eyes as she stepped over the threshold and felt the coldness in the house. She had no memory of the house ever feeling like this. Her grandmother's cheery greeting was missing, the stove was empty and the fireplace was vacant and gray.

Taking a deep breath, Brijit led Weylon and Nestariel into the small house.

"Brijit, are you sure you don't want to wait outside?" Weylon asked gently. "We don't know what we will find."

"No. She is my grandmother; it is my responsibility to –" Brijit gasped suddenly as she saw her grandmother lying on the kitchen floor.

"Grandmamma," she cried as she rushed forward. Weylon reached for her but wasn't fast enough to stop her.

Her grandmother lay on her back, her lifeless eyes were wide open and staring up at the ceiling. But it was the expression of horror on her face that shook Brijit more than anything. Whatever had killed her grandmother had been terrifying. A sob slipped passed Brijit's lips. "No, no, no," she murmured as she knelt beside her grandmother's body.

Suddenly a low menacing growl filled the air. Weylon jerked Brijit away just as Rufus lunged at her, spitting.

Before either of them could react, a dagger pinned the animal to the ground. Brijit looked up in horror to see Nestariel staring down at the still twitching body.

"Why did you do that?" Weylon asked angrily.

"Because the creature was obviously feral and infected."

"Not feral," Brijit protested, tears choking her words. "That was Rufus, my grandmother's cat."

Nestariel looked down at the body of the cat in doubt. "Are you certain?"

Brijit looked at the dead animal. Rufus had been a black cat identical to this one, but his eyes had been green not bright red. Still, the telltale white stripe on his chest gave him away.

"That's definitely Rufus." Brijit paused. Or it was what remained of Rufus. "He's changed somehow."

"Infected by whatever killed your grandmother," Nestariel noted.

Dread filled Brijit's chest as she looked at the twitching animal on the ground. It bore little resemblance to the house cat that loved to dig his claws playfully into her knee as he purred loudly enough to fill a room. This thing was grotesquely twisted, its dead eyes still holding the look of evil that permeated from it. It was eerily similar to the creature that had attacked Weylon in the dead wood.

Was this what the evil did to living things it infected? Brijit shuddered as she thought of the poison that was still coursing through Weylon's body. She looked over at him but he bore no resemblance to the creature on the floor. He stood and looked around the room, his hand on the hilt of his sword, clearly searching for any sign of what had done this to her grandmother and Rufus.

Nestariel let out a dismissive grunt. "Whatever it was is long gone now," she told him. "Such evil can't linger in a town like this one. It is too full of the good, honest people of Five Corners. The evil of The Rift can't survive far from its roots – it can only invade for a short time before it is dispersed. At least for the present time. I fear there will come a time when such evil will run free in Five Corners, but that time has not yet arrived."

"This is my fault," Brijit whispered as tears filled her eyes. It was true. Nestariel had told her that when she used the magik in the dead wood, the evil had found the way to her grandmother.

"You couldn't have known, child," the Elder woman said softly.

Weylon rounded on the old woman. "Why would you say that? How could this have been Brijit's fault? She wasn't anywhere near here when this happened."

Nestariel gave Brijit a knowing looking and then pressed her lips together.

Brijit looked up from her grandmother's broken form on the floor and saw the confusion in Weylon eyes. "I know it's hard to believe but it's true, Weylon. This is my fault."

Weylon shook his head, still not understanding.

Nestariel looked at her grandmother's body and then around the small cottage with the drying herbs hanging from the ceiling, the crystals on the table in the corner and the books of magik lining the walls. She strode over to the shelves that held the books and began to examine them. She looked over her shoulder to where Weylon was standing, a look of confusion on his face.

"Brijit's grandmother was more than a simple wise woman, Weylon. Look around this dwelling…what do you see?"

It only took thirty seconds before Brijit saw the understanding dawn on Weylon's face. He turned to Brijit.

"What is she talking about?" She could see that he needed confirmation of what he already knew. Brijit remembered how he had reacted when he had seen the mark on Ana's child.

She bit her lip and said nothing. She knew she owed him an explanation, but she just couldn't explain what had happened in the forest that day. She couldn't bear to see the disappointment in his eyes when he realized that she was the granddaughter of a *Kurunii.*

"Brijit did what she had to in order to save your life, Weylon. She meant well."

He turned to Nestariel. "And what exactly did she have to do so save me, Nestariel?"

Suddenly she felt Weylon's hands on her shoulders, turning her to face him.

"Brijit?" He sounded hurt and confused.

Closing her eyes, Brijit weighed her options. Nestariel knew what she was and the chances were that the Elders also knew. Weylon deserved to know as well.

She looked up and met his brown eyes. Swallowing Brijit said, "I am *Kurunii* as was my grandmother before me."

Weylon gasped and stepped away, his face filled with horror.

"You mean you delve in…" his words trailed away as understanding dawned in his eyes. "What exactly did you do to save me, witch?"

#

Weylon built a pyre behind the house. His anger had threatened to bubble over after Brijit had admitted that she had used magik to save him. He had heard stories over the years of those who had been saved by such means. The stories never had happy endings.

Despite his anger, he had seen the misery on Brijit's pretty face and against his will he had felt a sense of pity toward her. But he still had to live with the choices she had made for him in that dark wood.

He closed his eyes as he remembered the darkness that had pushed him down and threatened to consume him after he had been attacked. It was pure evil. Even now he could remember how desperately he had fought against it. And then there had been nothingness until he had awoken at Tèarmann.

He still didn't understand exactly what Brijit had done to him. He hadn't waited around for an explanation after she confirmed that she had used witchcraft to save him. Witchcraft was also tainted with the dark. Whatever Brijit had done, Weylon knew that you couldn't cast out one kind of evil with another. Regardless of what Brijit had hoped, she should have known this.

The *Kurunii* were a dying breed in Five Corners. And he believed it was a good thing. Over the years, the women had steadfastly refused to work with Elders, *Coimirceoirí*, or the *Draíodóir*. They insisted that the work they did was different and sacred; that women had been wielding such magik for eons. But Weylon didn't believe it. Where there were *Kurunii* there was always trouble.

He was still overcome by the revelation that Brijit was of the ancient order of the *Kurunii*, the women who for millennium had been both feared and revered in the Five Corners. The sisterhood of witches. Why had she hidden it from him?

Suddenly the fact that Brijit had been able to save him when by everyone's account it should have been impossible made sense. But the *Kurunii* were known to delve deeply in the dark magik. While the women who were part of the order were generally good and helped those in Five Corners to live well, they also were not beyond engaging in the dark arts when they felt it was necessary. The only way Brijit could have saved him was to use magik.

All at once his certainty that the Elders had been mistaken when they said he was infected with the dark wasn't so strong. If Brijit had used dark magik to save him, then it was all too possible that Suiadan had been right and the evil that had infected him was not gone. What that meant for his future he didn't know.

But why did he feel so much better since the attack? It was as if the poison had given him strength and good health.

To have been infected by the poison of The Rift was one thing but to have it eradicated by another black magik could not be good. And Brijit had done it without his permission. She had chosen for him.

Anger started to bubble deep in his stomach. Finishing the pyre, he straightened and returned to the house to collect Brijit's grandmother's body. He ignored the tears and hurt on Brijit's face. He would not let himself feel anything for her pain.

He hoisted the dead woman in his arms and tried to forget that the woman he was carrying to the pyre had once been a *Kurunii*, a powerful one if she'd been able to somehow help Brijit wield magik from Jirgen Forest. Weylon shook his head as he placed her body on top of the wood he had collected. Burning her body was the only way to eradicate her evil from Five Corners.

Although that evil clearly still lingered in her granddaughter. And now, perhaps, it also lingered in him.

Nestariel and Brijit had followed him to the pyre. The Elder tossed the body of the small black cat onto the wood as well. Weylon met her gaze, but she just raised her eyebrows at him and then instructed him to light the pyre.

"We must burn the bodies to cleanse this area," she told them.

Weylon eagerly lit the pyre. He heard Brijit sob and resisted the urge to go to her. He would not look at her. He would not feel sorry for her. He would not forgive her.

Except every time he heard one of her sobs, it felt like a piece of his soul was tearing. Despite everything that had been revealed on this trip, the fact remained that Brijit had lost her only surviving relative, and she was clearly distraught. Even with all he had learned about her origins, Weylon couldn't help feel her pain as if it were his own. Brijit was still Brijit, and she was hurting. He wanted to go to her but something deep inside held him back.

The flames rose up, consuming the wood and inching closer and closer to her grandmother's body. Brijit turned away and shook her head. "I can't watch this," she whispered.

Nestariel stepped forward. "Come with me, Brijit. Weylon, see that the ashes are buried."

He nodded and watched them go back to the house.

He looked back at the flames that were now licking at her grandmother's black dress. Drawn by a fascination he could not explain, he crept closer to the fire. In a burst of hot energy, the grandmother's body was suddenly engulfed in white flames that had him stepping back a foot. As he continued to watch the fire, the body of the cat rolled off the pyre. And landed near his feet.

Take it, a dark voice whispered.

Weylon jerked and looked around, but he was alone. He shook his head, sure he must be imagining things. He looked back to where the dead animal lay on the ground.

Take it. You know you want it, the voice urged again. *Yes, feast on it.*

Without conscious thought Weylon found himself bending down to examine the remains of the dead cat. He should have just thrown it back on the pyre, but the voices were calling to him.

Taste it! Take it! You want it. You need it. The whisperings were dark and hungry, growing louder by the moment.

He glanced to the house and saw no sign of Nestariel or Brijit. *Taste the power of it! It is yours. You know it is!*

Suddenly lunging forward, Weylon pulled the cat's body from the ground and sank his teeth into it, sucking hard. The metallic, salty blood whetted his appetite and he drank deeply, feeling a surge of power and energy jolt through him.

All at once, Weylon pulled away and looked at the blood dripping on his hands. The whisperings in his head were gone. As horror filled him, he threw the cat's body back onto the pyre and ran down the hill to a small pond just out of sight of the house. He doused his head and hands in the water. Gagging, Weylon pulled his head out of the water and stared at his fractured reflection.

What was happening to him?

Chapter Fourteen

They stayed at Brijit's grandmother's house for two more days. Nestariel wanted to pack up all Grandmamma's books and scrolls. She sent Weylon into town to find a wagon and horse they could buy to transport the things back to Tèarmann.

Brijit spent the time going through the rest of her grandmother's belongings. Most of the things her grandmother had kept were practical. Beyond the copious scrolls and books that Nestariel insisted on taking, her grandmother had kept few personal things.

Brijit packed up the meager supply of food and clothing, and donated them to needy townsfolk in Evendel. Nestariel suggested that she not empty and sell the house but pack it up tight.

"You never know when you may have need of the dwelling, my dear."

Brijit didn't think she would ever have need of her grandmother's home. As Coimirceoirí she was destined to spend the rest of her days with the Elders. She didn't see how the house in Evendel would ever be useful to her.

"We never know what will happen in the future," Nestariel said softly, and something in her tone made Brijit agree with her. At least for now. She could always sell the house in the future. As a chosen *Coimirceoirí* she had little need for money anyway.

Weylon returned from the town with a strong horse and a sturdy wagon. Nestariel instructed them to begin packing the books and scrolls into it at once. Brijit watched Weylon as they worked together. His jaw was set, and she could feel the anger radiating from him. Her stomach churned. She longed to explain to him what happened, but one look at the stony expression on his face told her he wasn't in the mood to listen to her.

She sighed and returned to the house for an armful of scrolls. When she brought them out to the wagon, he turned on her.

"I suppose you want these so you can continue studying the black arts," he snarled, and Brijit recoiled as if struck.

"No!" she protested.

Weylon just shook his head and turned back to the half-full wagon bed.

"Why don't you believe me when I say I have no interest in these things?"

He looked down at her. "You're unreal. You are *Kurunii* and according to Nestariel your grandmother has one of the most complete libraries of magikal books that she's seen in all of Five Corners. It all belongs to you now." He gestured toward the piles of books and scrolls neatly stacked in the wagon. "I would think you couldn't wait to get your hands on them."

Brijit felt her chin quiver, but she took a deep breath, willing the tears to stay away. "I have never taken an interest in my grandmother's books."

"Oh, really? So what you did in the wood just came naturally?" he spat at her, his anger radiating from him.

"No! I didn't know what to do, Weylon. You were dying and I was desperate."

"So you decided magik would be the way to heal me?"

Brijit stepped back. "I didn't think about it. I called to my grandmother because she was the most gifted healer I had ever known. I thought if I could contact her, then maybe she would tell me how I could heal you."

He was staring at her in horror.

"What?"

He shook his head, "You were able to contact her here from Jirgen Forest?"

Slowly Brijit nodded.

He was looking at her with disgust in his eyes now. "You're even more powerful than I thought. No wonder the Elders want to keep you under their noses."

The tears were hovering on her eyelashes. Brijit blinked rapidly; she would not let them fall. "I was desperate for help to heal you, Weylon."

His tone was nasty as he spat, "And your grandmother was happy to give you that help, wasn't she?"

"No!" Brijit was shouting now. "No, she wasn't. She said I should let you die, okay? I chose to save you because I –" she broke off before she finished the sentence. *Because I love you.*

Brijit looked at him. His dark eyes were almost black with his raging emotions. He was beyond understanding. "The Elder knights wanted to kill you on the spot."

"And you should have let them," Weylon snapped.

Brijit felt as if she had been slapped. The tears spilled over, splashing hotly down her cheeks. Maybe he was right. Maybe she should have let him die.

"I couldn't," she whispered.

Weylon jumped down from the wagon and stood in front of her. "And why couldn't you, Brijit? Was it because you thought my life would be better to live like this, with this darkness in me? Did you think we would be even better partners if I had a touch of evil to match your own?"

"No!" Brijit shook her head in denial taking a step back from him. She hadn't thought any such thing. "I didn't even know my grandmother's cure involved the use of magik."

"Really?" Weylon sounded skeptical. "Come on, you're not as stupid as you like to pretend you are."

"She told me I would find mushrooms growing in the woods, and then she told me how to cook them into a brew that would save you."

"And you didn't question that? You knew that nothing grows in Jirgen Forest. And you'd seen enough to question anything that did grow there."

Brijit looked at her feet. He was right. She had known just how dead that wood had been, how devoid of life, and yet she hadn't questioned it. She had trusted her grandmother, and she had been desperate to save Weylon. She had been thankful to find the mushrooms and to be able to save him. And now he hated her for it. She looked at him sadly.

"I…I'm sorry, Weylon."

"Saying sorry doesn't make this better. I still have to live with this…" he pounded his chest, "this *thing* inside me. Do you have any idea how that feels?"

Brijit just stared at him. She had no words. She didn't really know how it felt. But she could guess. She had been inside Weylon's head, if only for a few moments, and it had been horrible.

If she had known he wished to die, she would have let him. At least she thought she would have. But then again, maybe she wouldn't have. Maybe she couldn't have.

He shook his head in disgust. "Stay away from me," he said and then turned and walked away.

Brijit let the tears fall then. It seemed that everything she was trying to do only ended up in failure. And saving Weylon seemed to be her biggest failure so far.

Chapter Fifteen

Ten days after they returned to the fortress, Princess Neirdre went into labor. Brijit and Erulassë were with her.

As is often the case with a first child, the birthing was not easy. It was made more difficult by Princess Neirdre's almost constant complaints. "It hurts," she moaned to Brijit as the contractions gripped her body.

"I know," Brijit murmured as sympathetically as she could while she rubbed the writhing princess's back. "Try to breathe."

"Make it stop!" Princess Neirdre moaned instead, swatting at Brijit's hands. "You stupid, *Coimirceoirí*, I thought you were supposed to help."

Brijit pushed away the annoyance that sprang up in her heart. "I can't make it stop," she told Princess Neirdre patiently, "but it will be easier if you breathe and calm yourself."

Princess Neirdre pushed Brijit's away again. "I can't calm myself. It hurts, it hurts. Make it stop!" she sobbed.

Brijit sighed. She had helped her grandmother birth many children over the years and had even delivered many on her own, but she had never seen a new mother fight so hard against bringing a baby into the world. *Except Ana*, a little voice in her mind reminded. Brijit shook her head. The girl in the small village had seemed to have good reason for not birthing her son. She had wanted to protect him. Neirdre seemed to just want the entire birthing process to be over.

"It will go easier for you if you relax," Brijit said reasonably, knowing that this was just the start of Princess Neirdre's labor. Princess Neirdre had many more hours to get through as her body prepared to deliver the next heir to the Elders. "Soon you will be holding your little baby in your arms. But for now you need to focus."

"You're stupid. I thought you would help. Mother, make it stop," she screamed at Erulassë. The older Elder woman looked shocked at her daughter's outburst and edged away from the bed toward the door with an expression of disgust on her face.

Clearly the older woman was not comfortable with the birthing process. Brijit wondered under what circumstances she had given birth to her own child. Neirdre had suggested that the Elder woman had been given a sleeping potion and missed the whole thing. Brijit didn't approve of such a practice. She believed, as her grandmother had taught her, that to not be present to the birthing process was akin to giving up your power as a woman. The birthing had a way of changing a woman, of helping her to recognize her own power. But Princess Neirdre didn't seem interested in that at all. She wanted to dissociate herself from the entire situation.

"Please, try to calm yourself," Brijit said again, fearing that Neirdre was tiring herself out before she needed to.

The door to the chamber suddenly opened and Nestariel entered. Erulassë took the opportunity to slip out behind her sister and disappear down the hallway. Neirdre was so livid when she saw her aunt that she didn't noticed her own mother abandoning her. Or perhaps she was used to it.

"Make her leave!" she screamed, as Nestariel approached her bed. "Get that witch out of here."

Brijit flinched for a moment before she realized that Neirdre was referring to her aunt. While Nestariel and Weylon knew of her status as *Kurunii*, Brijit had kept that knowledge from Neirdre and others at the fortress. She didn't think it would do any good for Neirdre to know about it before the birth of her child.

Nestariel was unperturbed by her niece's outburst. She merely smiled. "I might be a witch, but I seem to be the only one who can help you since you will not listen to Brijit."

Brijit stared at Nestariel. Was that why the older woman had not been overly surprised nor had she seemed concerned that Brijit was *Kurunii*. Was Nestariel a sister *Kurunii*? She remembered how Neirdre had referred to her aunt as a sorceress the first day Brijit had met her.

Nestariel ignored Princess Neirdre's curses and came forward, adjusting the pillows that were supporting the girl. "If you prop her more upright," Nestariel explained to Brijit as she adjusted the bedding around Neirdre much to the girl's ire, "you'll find you can lessen her pains." She moved her without heeding the howls of outrage that were emanated from her niece.

Once the older woman had finished, Neirdre calmed. She looked at her aunt in surprise. "How did you do that?"

Nestariel shook her head and ignored her question. "You need to stop spitting like a cat and conserve your energy, child," she said not unkindly. Then she set about removing the kettle from the fire and adding hot water to a brew she brought. "Drink this, it will help."

Princess Neirdre took the cup hesitantly from Nestariel. She took a sniff of the brew and made a face. "I'm not drinking that," she said in disgust holding the cup away from her.

"It will ease your pains," Nestariel told her.

A strong contraction took hold of Neirdre then, and she moaned loudly and then swallowed the tea down with several noisy gulps.

Through the long hours of the night, Princess Neirdre's pain was controlled in large part by Nestariel. At times Brijit wondered why she was even there, but when she tried to leave the room both Neirdre and Nestariel protested.

As the early hours of the morning inched toward dawn, Neirdre's pain became more regular until she started to moan, "I need to push."

Nestariel looked at Brijit. "Get ready, the time has come."

An hour later, the baby began to emerge. Neirdre collapsed, spent and exhausted, as Brijit caught the child in her arms.

"Let me see her," Neirdre murmured after a moment. "The next great leader of our people. Minathrial, my daughter."

But Brijit did not hand the child to the mother. Instead she looked at Nestariel not knowing what to say.

"What is wrong, child?" Nestariel demanded as she came around to where Brijit cradled the wailing babe.

Brijit met her eyes. "It is a boy!"

#

Princess Neirdre refused to hold her son. When Nestariel tried to convince her that cuddling the child would ensure bonding, she started screaming hysterically.

"I don't want to bond! He was supposed to be a girl. He was supposed to be the next great leader. I don't want a boy! I want the girl I was promised."

As her screams escalated, Nestariel pushed Brijit toward the door. Brijit backed out of the room with the swaddled babe in her arms. He screwed up his tiny face and began howling almost as loud as his mother. Brijit lifted the babe to her chest.

"Shhh, there, there. It will be okay," she whispered to the small bundle as she gently patted his back. The baby suddenly stopped crying. Brijit looked down at him and saw he was watching her, his eyes a surprisingly clear green for one so young.

She told the Elder girl who had followed her out of the room to bring her a large basin of warm water and some towels. When she returned, Brijit unswaddled the babe and set to washing the mucus and blood from his tiny form, marveling at how perfect his pale skin was. As she cradled him in the water, Brijit couldn't help smiling as his eyes slowly drifted shut. He was going to fall asleep in the warm water. A true angel.

She let him rest for a few moments and then turned him to wash his back. Brijit's breath left her. On the left shoulder of the tiny boy, was a mark that was all too familiar. A triquetra. Fear for this tiny creature suddenly filled her. Would they kill a royal child, based on the mark? Brijit did not think so. But after what had happened to the little girl in Merryville and Ana's halfling newborn, Brijit couldn't help feeling fearful for the small boy in her arms.

She studied the baby for a few moments longer. While he might be doomed to not be the next great leader of the Elders, this child was exceptionally beautiful. Even as an infant his bone structure and coloring were that of Elder royalty.

Her heart twisted as she realized that his mother had rejected him without giving him a second glance. Tears pricked at her eyes. No child deserved to be shoved aside by his mother. What kind of parent would do such a thing? What would Princess Neirdre do if she knew about the triquetra?

Straightening, Brijit tried to think of a plan to protect this baby. She wondered what Weylon would do. Quietly she asked the servant girl to find her fellow *Coimirceoirí.*

Weylon and her had not spoken since they left her grandmother's house. She knew that he preferred it that way, but Brijit didn't know who else to turn to right now. Weylon was the only one who knew about the mark and the dead children. And they were both sworn guardians of the royals. He might not want to deal with her, but she knew he took his duties as a *Coimirceoirí* seriously.

Together they could surely come up with a plan to protect him.

Weylon froze in the doorway when he saw the baby, now swaddled and cradled in Brijit's arms as she sat in the chair in the corner of her room. She looked up at him.

He cocked his head, his face filled with confusion. "Why is the royal heir here with you?" His tone was cold.

Brijit looked down at the sweet babe sleeping and sighed. "It's a boy."

Weylon froze halfway across the room.

"The princess refuses to even see him."

He looked at her in surprise.

"And there's more..." She paused and unwrapped the blanket swaddling the child.

Weylon's face paled when he saw the mark on the baby's shoulder. Brijit knew he must be thinking about Ana's son.

"Who has seen it?" he asked gruffly.

Brijit shook her head. "Only me. For now,"

He nodded thoughtfully.

"Weylon, what are we going to do?"

#

An hour later, Brijit found herself outside the Crown Prince's chambers. Weylon and her had come to the conclusion that Princess Neirdre was not the only parent the little babe had. Surely his father would not reject him.

As for the triquetra, they had agreed to keep that to themselves for now. Weylon didn't think the Crown Prince would let any harm come to his son, but they decided to wait and see what his reaction to the child was before they showed him the mark on his son's shoulder.

Brijit, herself, didn't know what that mark could mean on the children. Why was the ancient mark of the sisterhood suddenly appearing on newborn children? She feared that black magik had been used to produce it, but she had no proof of that nor did she have any idea why that would be the case. Even if the *Kurunii* had some role to play in the mark appearing, Brijit didn't know what that was or what purpose it served. And until she learned more, she didn't think it would be wise to share her worries with anyone else.

Suiadan was in his private rooms awaiting news of his wife and child. When Brijit was led into his room by the two Elder sentinels who stood guard outside his chambers, the Crown Prince stopped his pacing and turned to her, concern clear on his features.

"I've brought your son to meet you," Brijit said, her eyes on his face waiting to see his reaction, hoping it would not mirror that of Neirdre.

But Suiadan took the news of a son far better than his young wife had.

His lips parted in surprise. "A son?"

Brijit nodded and held the child out to him. Suiadan sat in the armchair in the corner of the room and held his hands up to receive the child. His surprise faded to pleasure as she placed the boy in his arms.

"His name will be Meldiron," he said firmly. "My son." He gazed down in wonder at the now quiet babe who was looking right back at him. From Suiadan's reaction, Brijit could see it was love at first sight. She smiled, relief coursing through her.

"Sir," Brijit hesitated, not knowing how to tell him of his wife's reaction to the baby's gender.

He looked up at her, his green eyes calm. "My wife is displeased?"

"She won't even look at him, never mind hold him." Brijit paused and bit her lip, wondering how to bring up the awkward subject of feeding Prince Meldiron. The baby turned his head and began rooting at the Crown Prince's tunic. When it yielded nothing, he screwed up his little face and let out an angry yowl.

"Your son will need to eat," Brijit pointed out the obvious.

Suiadan laughed and nodded. He seemed unsurprised. Then he called one of his men to him and spoke to him quietly. A few minutes later a woman with a babe of about two months strapped to her chest appeared.

"Aranel, Princess Neirdre and I have been blessed with a son."

She bowed in a deep curtsy. "Congratulations, my liege."

"We are in need of a wet nurse." He looked at her meaningfully. "Would you be willing to serve in such a capacity?"

"It would be my honor," she murmured, unfastening her own son from her chest and handing him to Brijit before taking the now wailing Meldiron from the Crown Prince. She sat in the armchair in the corner and expertly latched him onto her breast without hesitation or embarrassment. The child suckled hungrily.

"He is a strong boy," Suiadan said with approval. "He will make a great Crown Prince one day."

Brijit smiled and settled Aranel's child onto some blankets near his mother's feet before she left the chamber. She was happy that at least one of the child's parents saw him as a blessing, and Aranel seemed to be honored to serve in the position of royal wet nurse.

Brijit realized that she would have to speak to the woman alone. She doubted the Crown Prince would discover the mark on the child's shoulder, but she was sure Aranel would see it soon enough. The moment the nurse bathed the young prince she would see the triquetra. Brijit had to ensure that that mark on the royal heir's shoulder remained a secret…at least for now.

Chapter Sixteen

Brijit found the royal nurse in her new chambers. The Crown Prince had Aranel and her son moved to rooms adjoining his own so he could see Meldiron whenever time allowed. The woman welcomed Brijit into her room with a smile.

"Would you like to hold him, *Coimirceoirí*?" she asked shyly as she finished feeding the young prince.

Brijit smiled and nodded, holding her arms out to take the small baby. He looked up at her with those incredibly green eyes again and then, milk drunk, he slowly closed them and fell asleep.

"He is a very good baby," Aranel told her. "And I'm not just saying that because he's the future Crown Prince. He's much better than Samred." The words were not unkind, and Aranel had a smile in her voice as she cradled her own son in her arms. "This one is a little monkey," she confided.

Brijit looked at Aranel. The Elder woman looked at ease and happy.

"Is caring for two babies too much?" she asked.

Aranel shook her head. "No. I'm happy to help. And Samred will enjoy the company as he gets older."

It was true. Meldiron and Aranel's son would likely become good friends as they entered boyhood. Unless Princess Neirdre changed her feelings toward her son, Brijit didn't think that Meldiron would have a mother figure other than Aranel. She looked down at the sleeping boy. It was such a shame. He was a sweet baby and she had no doubt that he would grow into a sweet boy.

Brijit returned her attention to Aranel and saw how at ease she was with her own son as well.

"Samred is not your first son?" Brijit asked.

Aranel looked up in surprise and then laughed. "Oh, no, my lady. Samred is my last baby. I have three others, all half-grown back in Séreméla."

Brijit wondered how Aranel had come to be at Tèarmann when she had a family back in Séreméla.

As if reading her mind, the woman answered, "You realize that it wasn't wholly unexpected that the princess would reject her child. Even if she had birthed a girl, many doubted that she would nurse her own child. I was brought along under the pretense of being a kitchen maid, but I had a suspicion all along that the Crown Prince might call on me to take the honor of feeding his child."

Brijit nodded. So Suiadan understood his wife better than she had given him credit for.

"Royal marriage aren't like others," Aranel told her when she saw the expression on Brijit's face. "Try not to judge Neirdre too harshly. She was chosen as princess not out of love but because her family had the right connections and she was young and beautiful. Prince Suiadan wanted to have a mate who would give him strong and healthy children." Aranel wrinkled her nose, "Not the most ideal conditions for starting a marriage, but it is tradition."

"You mean not all Elder marriages are like that?"

Aranel laughed at those words. "No, Brijit. Most Elders marry for love. It is only the royals who are stuck marrying out of duty."

Brijit shook her head. It appeared the Elder traditions affected not just Coimirceoirí but others in the realm as well. She looked down at Prince Meldiron again. She couldn't deny that the marriage had produced a beautiful son. She thought of the mark on his shoulder and became serious.

"Aranel," she said as casually as she could, "have you bathed the baby yet?"

The wet nurse looked Brijit in eye, "I have, Coimirceoirí."

A look of understanding passed between them. "Has anyone else seen it?"

"No."

"I think it would be best if it stayed that way," Brijit said softly.

"I think you are right, *Coimirceoirí.*"

#

"The young prince is doing well despite my niece's rejection of him?"

Brijit was in Nestariel's chambers with the small baby in her arms. Neirdre continued to refuse to the see her son, and Brijit wanted Aranel to have some time with her own child. She had taken to collecting Prince Meldiron each afternoon and giving the nurse a few hours to herself in her chambers.

This was the first time she had brought Meldiron to his great-aunt's chambers, and she had seen the way both Nestariel and Eöl Ar-Feiniel looked at the little prince. With twin expressions of pure enchantment. She hid a smile.

"Would you like to hold him?" she asked Nestariel.

The Elder raised her eyebrows. "Well, if you need a rest, I suppose I could."

Brijit played along. She hadn't missed the eagerness in Nestariel's eyes.

"It suits you, A'maelamin," Eöl Ar-Feiniel said quietly as he watched the Elder woman cradling the small babe.

Brijit hid her surprise at his easy use of the Elder term of endearment. Nestariel ignored him, her attention completely captured by the child in her arms. Brijit couldn't help wondering why Eöl Ar-Feiniel and Nestariel had never married and had children of their own. She had spent enough time with them to see how strongly they cared about one another.

But she felt it was probably a story for another time. She turned her attention to another question that had been bothering her since the prince's birth.

"Nestariel," she began softly, not wanting to intrude on Nestariel's time with her new great-nephew but also knowing that it was the perfect situation to ask her questions. The Elder would not be able to deflect her and run away.

"Hmmm," she looked up from the babe in her arms.

"I want to ask you something, and I hope you will be honest with me."

Nestariel's dark-green eyes narrowed slightly. "Say your piece, *Coimirceoirí*."

Brijit bit her lip. Obviously Nestariel suspected that what she had to ask was not going to be pleasant.

"Princess Neirdre has called you a few things that have me wondering…"

"What did my niece call me?"

"Well a sorceress…and a witch." Nestariel raised her eyebrows. Brijit hurried on, "I was just wondering if…"

The Elder's eyes softened. "You were wondering if I'm *Kurunii* as your grandmother was."

Brijit nodded.

Sympathy filled her lined face. "No, my child, I am not."

Disappointment washed over Brijit. She had hoped that with her grandmother now gone there would be at least one other person she could trust and ask question about the *Kurunii*.

"But you took the scrolls and books."

Nestariel nodded. "Yes, to help with the translation, my dear," she nodded to where Eöl Ar-Feiniel's desk was covered with papers.

The old man nodded. "Yes, the witch lore does help with the translation a bit," he acknowledged.

"Elders have never been *Kurunii*, Brijit. The witch sisters are wholly human. I'm sorry, child."

There it was again. First, Weylon had hinted that the Elders were not human, and now Nestariel was suggesting the same thing. What could it mean?

But Brijit wasn't getting any answers today. Nestariel had turned back to the child in her arms. The conversation was over.

#

A week later, Brijit wandered into Nestariel's room again, hoping to get some answers about the *Kurunii* from the Elder woman. While Nestariel was not *Kurunii* herself, she surely knew about the history of witches in Five Corners. Because Brijit had missed that part of her studies at the Academy, her knowledge was rudimentary at best.

And as she came to accept the truth of what Grandmamma had been, of what she was a part of, the more she longed to know about her heritage. More important, she wanted to figure out if being *Kurunii* born would affect her as a *Coimirceoirí*. She was sure Nestariel would have some answers for her.

It was only when she was halfway across the main room in Nestariel's chambers that she realized the Elder woman was not there. Eöl Ar-Feiniel looked up from his work and smiled at her.

"Hello, Brijit! Always good to see you, my dear."

Brijit nodded absently. "Nice to you as well, Eöl Ar-Feiniel," she came over to the desk where he was working. "Are you making any progress?"

He nodded with a gleam in his old eyes. "Always making progress, my dear. Always making progress. It might be slow but it is something."

Brijit sighed and looked at the papers on the desk.

"Is Nestariel not here?"

He shook his head. "She's been called to some meeting by the Crown Prince. I'm not sure how long she will be."

Disappointment filled Brijit but she nodded in understanding and turned to the door.

"You are welcome to wait here," Eöl Ar-Feiniel told her as he shuffled more of his papers around.

"Are you sure I'm not disturbing you?"

He shook his head. "Oh, no! I was just about to take a break. I've been meaning to visit with you, Brijit. I think that I could answer some questions you might have."

Brijit looked at him sharply. "Questions?"

"About the *Kurunii*. Surely, you must have questions." His old eyes were suddenly shrewd. "You do realize that as the chief archivist in Séreméla I have access to more information than almost anyone else in Five Corners."

Brijit stared at him.

"The *Kurunii* are an interesting group. They have existed for a very long time. Come and sit with me and I'll tell you what I know."

Brijit followed Eöl Ar-Feiniel to the small sitting area. He lowered himself into a chair and closed his eyes. "This place is tiring," he murmured. "I wish Nestariel would leave it and come back to Séreméla. She is hastening her own demise living this close to The Rift." He opened his eyes then and saw Brijit watching him. She wondered if he'd forgotten she was there.

"So the *Kurunii*. Yes, they have been in Five Corners since the beginning. You are part of an ancient order of women who have done much good in their time."

Brijit was surprised. "But then why do so many people fear and hate them."

Eöl Ar-Feiniel sighed. "Well, people tend to fear what is different and what they don't understand. And I'm afraid my people have helped to stoke the fear regarding both the *Kurunii* and the *Draíodóir.*"

Brijit stiffened at the mention of the order of druids.

"Ah, *Kurunii* are fine but you don't like the *Draíodóir*, Brijit?" Eöl Ar-Feiniel gave dry chuckle. "Be careful you don't fall into hypocrisy, my dear."

At Brijit's confused look, he softened.

"Forgive me. I forget that you are not privy to the knowledge I have. Let me start with the *Kurunii.* Tracing their origins is almost impossible because they have always been in Five Corners. At least as far back as recorded history goes. They were an order of women who wielded magik to heal and care for others."

"But if they always did good, then why is there such prejudice against them," Brijit asked.

A deep sadness washed over Eöl Ar-Feiniel's face. "That is partly the doing of the Elders." He closed his eyes and shook his head. "Too many innocent women were killed because of that prejudice, all started because of jealousy."

Brijit was surprised. What could the Elders be jealous of?

Eöl Ar-Feiniel read her thoughts. "Their ability to wield magik, my dear."

"But Elders have always been able to wield magik."

Eöl Ar-Feiniel nodded. "That is true, but not in the way you imagine." His brow furrowed and he seemed to be searching for words. "Come with me. I want to show you something."

Surprised, Brijit stood and followed him out to the hall. Without talking, he led her outside to a part of the fortress she had never been in before. "Come," he called back to her over his shoulder, his words carried away by a dry, hot wind.

He stopped on the ramparts facing westward and looked into the distance, worry and distaste on his face. "You see that?" he pointed.

Brijit followed his line of sight and saw a mass of never-ending darkness on the horizon. She swallowed back her fear and stared, wholly mesmerized.

"That, my dear, is The Rift. And it exists entirely because we have made it."

Chapter Seventeen

Brijit turned to Eöl Ar-Feiniel in horror. "We made it?" she looked at the way the brown sands ebbed into black as they got closer to The Rift. She remembered how the desert she had traveled over with the Elder knights had been completely barren of any living or growing thing. It was like everything was dead on it.

In the distance, the darkness swirled. Brijit instinctively stepped back from the edge of the rampart, her eyes filling with tears. How could they have made that much evil?

She turned back to Eöl Ar-Feiniel. "How?" she whispered.

The old man touched her arm gently. "Do you understand that even using a bit of magik is a great responsibility that has repercussions?" he asked softly.

Brijit paused. She hadn't thought of that. Her grandmother had not guided her in the use of magik, and it wasn't taught at the Academy. And yet deep down she knew that it wasn't something one wasted. You only used magik if all other means of remedy had failed. Her grandmother had taught her that, even if Brijit hadn't realized it at the time.

She nodded.

"Good, then you instinctively know what too many over the years have ignored and some are still ignoring."

He looked at the swirling evil in the distance once more and said, "Let's talk more inside."

Brijit was happy to leave that darkness behind. It seemed to her that it embodied the voices she had heard in Weylon's mind when she had entered it in Jirgen Forest. Dread filled her again, and she pulled her attention back to Eöl Ar-Feiniel who was striding ahead of her back to Nestariel's chambers.

Once there he put the kettle over the fire and turned back to her.

"Sit, Brijit. I will make some tea."

Brijit sat blindly, trying to make sense of what she had seen on the ramparts. The Rift was far more deadly and evil than anything she could have imagined. And Eöl Ar-Feiniel said they were responsible for it.

When she had a warm cup of mint tea in her hands, Eöl Ar-Feiniel sat across from her.

"I'm sorry to have upset you so much, Brijit, but it's important that you understand this. You, in particular, with the power that you possess."

She looked at him sharply.

"You are a *Kurunii* and a *Coimirceoirí*, Brijit. That particular blend has never been made before. And I would know if it had. The Elder Council had a very specific purpose in choosing you to be the *Coimirceoirí* of the royal family. I don't know what that purpose is, but I am sure your appointment was no accident."

"How did we make that…that evil, Eöl Ar-Feiniel?" Brijit burst out, unable to hold it in anymore.

The old Elder sat back in his chair and took a sip of his own tea. "Ah, that is an excellent question." He paused and studied her. "You do understand that when magik is used even for good, there is a discharge of negative energy."

Brijit furrowed her brow. She had never heard of such a thing.

Eöl Ar-Feiniel went on, "Think of it as payment for the use of magik. Each use costs a little – the price is a bit of darkness coming into the world."

Brijit didn't like where this conversation was leading.

"Now, that wasn't a big deal when there were few people wielding magik and it was used for valid reasons. A *Kurunii* might draw on the power to help with a particularly difficult healing or a *Draíodóir* might use it to shift the weather when a particularly harsh drought hit the land. And those uses were manageable. Some darkness was let in but it would disperse before more magik was used."

Brijit nodded. That made perfect sense.

"But it changed many generations ago. I'm ashamed to say that my people, in particular, learned how to use magik for their purposes. They learned that a little bit of magik would make the flowers bloom brighter or make their faces age slower. And so more and more Elders started using magik. But they did so without any thought as to the dark side of using magik. They thought that since they were using it for such small things, they didn't have to be careful." His green eyes filled with sorrow. "They were wrong."

"By the time Queen Aibhilín came to power, the damage had been done. The Rift was growing at a tremendous rate and the Western Sea was almost entirely dead. But magikal use wasn't checked. In fact, in Séreméla it was being used more and more. And as the use grew the more The Rift grew. It wasn't until The Rift was on the very borders of Séreméla that it got the notice of Queen Aibhilín and the Elder Council. At first the queen didn't believe that the Elders needed to change their lifestyle. Aibhilín herself was an excessive user of magik. Her lifestyle would have to change dramatically to even consider cutting out its use. And so instead of changing the lives of the people in Séreméla, she demanded that the people of Five Corners stop using magik."

Brijit gasped. "The *Kurunii* and the *Draíodóir*."

Eöl Ar-Feiniel nodded. "Yes, the very people who were using magik responsibly and for the good of all of Five Corners were the ones who were punished."

"But that wasn't fair."

Eöl Ar-Feiniel shook his snowy head. "No, but at that stage in her reign Aibhilín was more interested in keeping the Elders happy than considering what was good for all of Five Corners. As you can imagine, the *Kurunii* and the *Draíodóir* were not pleased with this ultimatum from Séreméla. At first they ignored it completely, but then both *Kurunii* and *Draíodóir* began to turn up dead. Aibhilín had ordered any who disobeyed her to be put to death."

Brijit shook her head, unable to believe the extent of Aibhilín's cruelty. And yet today the last Elder queen was spoken of as hero.

"The *Kurunii* and the *Draíodóir* could have joined together then to fight the Elders and history may have had a far different outcome, but they did not. Instead the *Draíodóir* decided to work with the Elders. They aligned themselves with Séreméla and, by doing so, they were able to obtain special magikal licenses that allowed them to still practice limited amounts of the dark arts. It wasn't long before their helpful use of magik to make lives better for those living in Five Corners was overtaken by the demands and needs of the Elders. For you see, while Elders could use magik, to a limited degree, they were not as powerful as the *Draíodóir*."

"What happened to the *Kurunii*?" Brijit asked.

"They went underground. Disguised themselves as wise women of the villages. The Elders may have suspected who they were, but the people of Five Corners worked together to keep the women safe." He paused and took a deep breath. "There was, of course, the occasional witch burning when a *Kurunii* was discovered, but for the most part that is how they continued."

"And Aibhilín? What happened to her?"

Eöl Ar-Feiniel smiled slightly. "Queen Aibhilín was able to redeem herself before the end. She came face to face with The Rift quite by accident. She had decided she wanted to enjoy what had once been the Elders' royal summer home on the Western Sea…"

"Tèarmann," Brijit murmured.

Eöl Ar-Feiniel nodded. "When she arrived here, she found the dead desert and The Rift at the doorstep of what had once been her royal family home. The *Draíodóir* who had accompanied her pointed out again that The Rift was the result of the ongoing excess of magikal use. Aibhilín was horrified. She returned to Sérémela and tried to convince her people to change their ways. But, of course, they resisted, unwilling to give up the lifestyles they had become accustomed to. Aibhilín tried to lead by example. She stopped all magikal use in her life, and she aged gracefully as an Elder queen should do. But still the people could not or would not follow her example. There were some, of course, who did cut back on their magikal use, but most Elders had become addicted to it. So Aibhilín, not knowing what else to do, returned to The Rift and bonded with it."

Brijit gasped.

"Yes, she gave up her live for her people and for Five Corners. It is said that she claimed she was not the Chosen One who would save her people but that she had bought them time. And with her last words she implored her people to change their ways."

Brijit shook her head, moved by such sacrifice. "Did they change their ways?"

Eöl Ar-Feiniel looked sad. "For a time, my people cut back on their use of magik. But today it is growing once again. And the magikal protection that was all that remained of Queen Aibhilín is now eroding. I fear it is only a matter of time before the darkness that makes up The Rift breaks free and all of Five Corners is lost."

Chapter Eighteen

Word of the child's birth and his gender spread quickly. No one in the fortress expressed disappointment out loud, but Weylon could feel it in the air. Many of the Elders, especially those at the fortress, had counted on a female heir being born. It was, after all, the reason they had left their home in Séreméla and fled to this godforsaken place. Now they were faced with the reality of yet another Crown Prince instead of a future queen. The mood at the fortress had darkened perceptibly. It was like a veil had fallen over the place.

Princess Neirdre, however, was the only one who dared to reject Prince Meldiron openly. Weylon's stomach churned as he tried to imagine a mother reacting in such a way to her child, especially right after birth. It was inconceivable.

But the fact that Suiadan seemed delighted with his son kept the people at Tèarmann from rebelling. Without exception it seemed that the Elders adored their ruling Crown Prince. Weylon had not heard anyone speak ill of him.

They were less enthralled with Princess Neirdre, it seemed. From the kitchen to the training field, Weylon heard murmurs of disgust whenever her name came up. Only when the Crown Prince was present was the princess referred to in polite terms. If Suiadan was aware of how his people felt toward his bride, he didn't let it show.

Weylon hadn't seen Brijit since the night of Meldiron's birth. While he had helped her that night, it hadn't been because she had asked him. He had only helped because it was his duty to the royal family. As far as he was concerned, Brijit could rot.

He still could not believe that she had used her dark magik on him. He didn't know if it was remnants of that dark magik or the poison from the creature that had attacked him that was affecting his mood, but more and more he found himself battling dark thoughts.

His mind kept turning back to what had happened at that funeral pyre in Evendel. Weylon couldn't explain what had come over him. But he hadn't been able to forget how he felt while feasting on the carcass of the dead cat. How power had surged through him, making him feel more alive than he had ever before.

And while that memory scared him, he would be lying if he didn't admit that it also fascinated him. A deep craving was growing within him for more of what he had feasted on. He pushed such urges away, disgust filling him whenever he became aware of them, but they continued to emerge at the most unexpected times.

There was a restlessness growing within him. He couldn't explain it. More and more he found himself on the ramparts looking to the West. The Rift called to him, but he didn't know what it called for or how he would answer it. Dark whispers filled his mind. *Come. Join us*, they taunted. Weylon knew that to leave the fortress and go out on the sands toward the darkness would be nothing short of suicide. But it called to him nonetheless, filling his dreams with dark, powerful images and whispering in the back of his mind at the most unexpected moments. *Come. There is nothing for you here. Come. Come play with us. Come join us*.

One morning when he was standing atop the fortress with the hot wind blowing in his face, he saw something that startled him. In the far distance, barely perceptible to his eye, there was movement. Something was coming from The Rift.

As he continued to watch, his eyes straining, he suddenly realized what he was seeing. Riders were coming from The Rift! Armed riders!

Without thinking, Weylon sounded the alarm. But he continued to watch as more and more of the black horses emerged from the darkness. They were still a great distance away when Weylon realized that there were men atop those horses.

Men lived in The Rift? The thought was unbelievable and…exciting. He had assumed that nothing could survive in that swirling darkness. Could it be that he had been wrong? His heart began to pound, and a dark smile touched his lips. The word *brothers* filtered through his thoughts. *Join us*, the whispers said again. But before he could process them, Suiadan was striding toward him with his personal guard. Weylon felt a pang of regret for raising the alarm.

As Suiadan approached, Weylon cleared his face of all expression. The Crown Prince swore under his breath when he saw the dark riders in the distance. He barked orders to his men in the Elder language before he turned back to Weylon.

"What are your plans?" Weylon asked him.

Suiadan remained silent. He watched the approaching riders for a moment before turning and starting down the stairs toward the stable. Weylon followed the Crown Prince.

They were in the stable before Suiadan answered Weylon's question. "We will go and meet them in battle," he said darkly, as if he had been expecting this development for some time.

Weylon nodded and made to saddle his own horse to join the Elders. An eagerness to meet those riders was filling him. Finally, he would be able to quench the desire that had filled him almost daily since leaving Evendel.

But the Crown Prince stopped him with a firm grip on his shoulder.

Weylon froze, not understanding. Then Suiadan spoke. "You will not be coming with us, Weylon Forborrow."

He looked at the Crown Prince in surprise and opened his mouth to protest.

"Putting you in this situation would be dangerous for you and for all of us. You are doing well, but you are not cured. Never forget that. You are not ready to meet with those that live in The Rift. You may never be ready for that challenge."

Weylon hid the hurt he felt at Suiadan's words. The Crown Prince had known that men lived in The Rift. He had known and kept it from him. Weylon felt a burst of anger, but he pushed it aside. This was his Crown Prince. Despite everything, he was *Coimirceoirí* first. His owed his allegiance to the royal family, regardless of that dark yearning inside him.

The Crown Prince looked at him steadily until Weylon broke eye contact, fearful that the he would be able to see a trace of what had happened at Brijit's grandmother's house in his eyes. He knew Suiadan was right. Weylon didn't trust himself to go out on the sands with the Elders. Now that the Crown Prince's serious face was in front of him instead of those dark riders on the sand, his sanity returned. He could not ride out with the Elders or he would be lost forever. He knew it was true. Despair filled him, and he cursed Brijit once again for resigning him to this fate. But Suiadan's next words caught his attention.

"And I have a more important job for you, besides."

He looked at the Crown Prince, hope replacing the despair he was feeling a moment before.

"You must take my wife and son to safety."

Weylon stared at Suiadan in surprise. He found it hard to comprehend. The Crown Prince was assigning him the task of keeping his family safe. Weylon knew how much that said about Suiadan's trust in him. The Crown Prince smiled at him.

"You are my *Coimirceoirí*, Weylon. I know you have pledged to keep my family safe. We have stationed a man in the Wastelands."

Weylon looked at Suiadan sharply. Finn had been sent to the Wastelands. Suddenly he understood. The Elders had obviously feared that something like this might happen. Finn had been sent ahead to prepare for such a situation.

Suiadan continued with his instructions, "You will take the women and the child and join him there. We will send word when it is safe to return. Do you understand?"

Weylon nodded, his blood beginning to pump with adrenaline. Those riders he had seen were heading for the fortress at a fast pace. They would be there in less than hour at that pace.

"Don't delay. Go now," the Crown Prince commanded as he hoisted himself onto his mount. "Remember, Weylon Forborrow, the future of the Elders rests with you." And with that he roared to his men and charged out the gates to do battle.

#

Weylon pounded on Princess Neirdre's door until Brijit opened it.

"We are under attack. The Crown Prince has ordered your evacuation." He looked into the room and saw the princess, Nestariel, and Erulassë.

"Where is the child?" he asked Brijit quietly.

"He is with Aranel." Brijit lowered her voice and looked back at Princess Neirdre, "She still refuses to see him."

"Can you get Aranel and the child prepared to flee? As soon as possible."

Fear filled Brijit's eyes but she nodded. "How soon?"

"Within fifteen minutes."

Horror flashed across her face, but she quickly hid it. He turned to go, but her voice stopped him. "Weylon, who is attacking us?"

He looked back at her.

"Don't ask questions now. Just get them to the stables as soon as possible. The Crown Prince is counting on me to keep his family safe."

Brijit nodded again but stepped from the room after him, carefully closing the door so the others would not hear them.

"How serious is this?"

Weylon frowned, not wanting to discuss this with her but realizing that there was no point hiding it. The sooner he explained, the more cooperative she would be. "The Crown Prince and his men have ridden out to defend the fortress against riders from The Rift."

Brijit gasped and turned pale. "From The Rift?"

Weylon nodded.

He felt her hand on his forearm suddenly and resisted the urge to pull away. "Are you okay?" she asked. Hatred boiled up inside him as he realized that she must have suspected that The Rift had been calling to him.

But Weylon had not known that anything lived there. If he had known about those riders earlier, he didn't like to think what he might have done. The days he'd spent on the ramparts looking into The Rift as the darkness called to him. Thinking about it made his knees weak, and it took all his willpower not to find his mount and ride out to meet them. But then he saw Brijit's anxious face looking up at him, and he shook the dark thoughts from his mind.

Now he did move his arm from beneath her hand. He ignored the softness that was in her touch, reminding himself that she was the reason he was tempted to turn his back on his duties. She was the one who had done this to him. She had cursed him with this life filled with temptation.

"I will meet you all in the stable in less than half an hour," he told her tersely, needing to put distance between them.

"Okay," she said softly, and as he started to stride away he heard her call to him, "Weylon."

He looked back at her. She met his gaze firmly.

"I love you. You know that right?"

He felt as if he'd been hit in the solar plexus. The emotion in those three words threatened to knock down the wall he had built between them. A forgotten part of him longed to take her in his arms and reassure her that all would be okay. That he cared for her as much as she cared for him.

But then the knowledge of what she had done to him came back and he shook his head at her. He realized that what he had once felt for Brijit was now dead. She had killed it when she had saved him in the dead forest.

"Get them ready – we are running out of time," he spat over his shoulder before he turned and strode down the hallway, the pounding of his boots almost drowning out her hurt gasp.

#

Brijit was surprised when they managed to have all gathered in the courtyard in less than twenty minutes. What she'd seen on Weylon's face when she'd told him she loved him had torn at her heart. But it was the pain that had propelled her forward, ensuring that she got the others to the stable in time.

Nestariel seemed to sense that something was happening. She had followed Brijit out the door only moments after Weylon left and questioned her.

"Riders from The Rift," was all Brijit had to say before the older woman got the others in motion.

Brijit had focused on collecting Meldiron and Aranel. The nurse had packed up her son and the prince faster than Brijit thought possible.

She didn't know what Nestariel had said to Princess Neirdre and her mother to get them to leave so quickly, but they were there and ready to go.

Weylon had secured a wagon to transport them. When Princess Neirdre saw Prince Meldiron in Brijit's arms she hissed in disgust and looked like she would argue. But Weylon spoke.

"The Crown Prince insisted that his son accompany us," he said loudly enough for her to hear.

She rolled her eyes and slouched down in the wagon, anger radiating from her. But she knew better than to disagree. Brijit knew that the royal couple had engaged in many heated arguments about Meldiron. She could not avoid hearing their raised voices when she came to Princess Neirdre's chambers in recent weeks. The Crown Prince had instantly fallen in love with his son and was displeased by Neirdre's continued rejection of him. When Neirdre had accused him of choosing his son over her a few weeks ago, Suiadan had answered smoothly. "My son is my life now. You need to accept that."

Brijit looked down at the sweet baby in her arms. His huge green eyes had become even more brilliant in the past few weeks and a wisp of blond hair now covered his head. His little hand closed around her finger as he gazed up at her. As the wagon started to roll, his eyes slowly closed. He was sweet by nature, and Brijit could not understand Neirdre's aversion to him. If she would just try to hold her son for a few minutes, Brijit was sure the baby would break down her continued resistance to being a mother. But Neirdre was unmovable.

Weylon mounted his horse and rode beside them.

"Brijit," he said urgently as he came up to her side of the wagon.

She looked up from Meldiron's peaceful face. Weylon was serious. "If they get close, duck down in the wagon. Stay safe."

Her heart twisted as she thought about what he was saying. She feared that if the dark riders came close, Weylon would be lost to her. She didn't think he would be able to withstand the draw from The Rift. From what she had seen of the place, it was pure evil. And Weylon had been infected by the darkness. She wondered if he suspected this as well, but there was no time to ask, so she just nodded in reply to his words. He needed her to at least show the pretense of believing they were safe. Then he gave the command to the driver to leave.

The women and babies in the wagon were accompanied by Weylon and three Elder knights, one driving the wagon and two flanking it. Weylon and the riders formed a protective barrier around the wagon and escorted it out of the courtyard. The Wastelands were now to become their refuge.

Chapter Eighteen

They had been traveling across the desert for several days when suddenly Brijit heard shouting and the sound of horses' hooves pounding into the ground.

Weylon rode by her side of the cart. "Stay down," he barked before riding out with the two Elders on horseback.

Brijit made sure everyone in the cart was down and then she peeked over the edge of the cart to see what was happening.

"I said, stay down," Weylon roared in the distance and Brijit lowered her head.

Neirdre was crying. "What is happening?"

Brijit shook her head. She couldn't tell from where she lay on the bottom of the cart. Prince Meldiron began to wail and Aranel's son joined in.

"Shhh, shhh," Aranel murmured to the terrified infants. She looked at Brijit in despair. Brijit took Meldiron in her arms. Instantly the prince calmed down and looked up at her in wonder. Aranel silenced her son by putting him on her breast. Soon the sound of a baby suckling filled the cart.

Outside Brijit could hear the clang of metal on metal as the Elders and Weylon engaged in battle. The sounds were far off in the distance. Annoyance filled Brijit at not being able to seen anything, but Prince Meldiron let out a little sound of distress at her tenseness. "It's okay," Brijit whispered to him, forcing herself to relax.

As the baby settled, she listened hard again, her eyes meeting those of Nestariel on the other side of the cart. The sounds of battle were fading in the distance. Weylon was leading the would-be attackers away. Relief flooded through Brijit. She smiled faintly at Neirdre who was looking a little less terrified.

Just as the women in the cart started to relax, the back of the cart swung open and a dirty grizzled man with only one leg and a wicked curved blade in his filthy hands fixed his crazed eyes on them.

"What have we here?" he chortled as he took in the occupants of the cart. His eyes flicked over each of them until they settled on Neirdre and the small crown on her head.

"An Elder princess and her entourage, I would guess," he looked greedily at Prince Meldiron and then Aranel's son. "And which one of these is the Crown Prince?" Quickly he grabbed Neirdre and yanked her out of the cart. "Get out. All of you."

Nestariel rose slowly but obeyed. Brijit followed her lead and stepped out with Meldiron cradled in her arms. Aranel followed, but Erulassë dissolved in hysterics.

"Get out, sister," Nestariel hissed, but Erulassë would not stop wailing.

"Shut her up," the man hissed. Brijit saw now that he was younger than she thought. And he had a wicked gleam in his eyes. "Git out!" he barked at Erulassë, but she didn't shut up, nor did she try to get out of the cart. Instead, she started to scream.

Lightning fast, the man swung his blade and sliced Erulassë's neck. As her hot blood pooled onto the sand before them, Neirdre fainted. While the bandit was distracted, Nestariel kicked him in his good leg. He yelled, cursing as he fell, the blade knocked from his hands. Brijit lunged for his fallen weapon grabbing it and standing in front of him, Prince Meldiron still cradled in her arms.

"Drop it!" A cold voice said.

Brijit turned and saw another grizzled man, this one with both legs and a wicked looking dagger in his hands. He held Aranel's son by one heel.

The terrified baby was wailing, and Aranel was sobbing. "Let him go! Let him go!" He backhanded Aranel across the mouth. She fell to the sand and did not get up.

This bandit was considerably younger than his companion. He looked at the babe he was holding and then at the one in Brijit's arms, weighing his options.

"One of these two is our new Crown Prince, I would suspect," he drawled. "Is it the one the *Coimirceoirí* is holding or the one the nurse was so distraught over?" he paused looking at each of them in turn. The only sound was Aranel's son's increasing wails. Impatience flared on his face.

"Kill 'em both," the bandit at Brijit's feet hissed.

"Good idea, old man." And before anyone could move he rammed his dagger deep into the wailing child's chest and threw his body on the ground, advancing toward Brijit.

White rage filled Brijit. "You will not have him." Her voice was one even she did not recognize. And before the bandit could step any closer to her, Brijit reached out with her power and invaded his mind.

He screamed and fell to sand, holding his head in both hands. Before he could recover, an Elder arrow pierced his heart. Brijit continued to cradle Prince Meldiron, tears flowing down her cheeks as Weylon leapt from his horse and severed the head from the one-legged man who was still cowering on the sand.

Chapter Nineteen

The settlement could be seen in the distance when the stench hit them. Brijit fought the urge to cover her nose, but Princess Neirdre didn't try to hit her disgust.

"What is that smell?" she asked in horror.

It was Nestariel who answered her. "That is what the dead sea smells like when the wind blows this way," the old Elder said, amusement in her eyes.

Neirdre looked at her aunt in disbelief, but Brijit's attention was captured by the collection of buildings she could see in the distance. Could it be that after twelve long days on the road they were finally at the safe haven?

Her question was answered before she could voice it. Their little caravan rolled to halt as a young man emerged from one of the buildings. Brijit recognized him from the ceremony at the Academy so long ago. He was a *Coimirceoirí* apprentice from Stone Mountain.

He studied them with a quizzical expression when he saw them. Then his eyes landed on Weylon, and his face split with a huge grin.

"Weylon!" he called and hurried over to where her fellow *Coimirceoirí* was dismounting.

"Finn!" Weylon answered and the two men embraced.

"What is going on?" Finn asked when they stepped apart. He looked over at the party that accompanied Weylon. Brijit imagined they looked quite the sight with their exhausted faces and tattered clothes. Tears rolled down Aranel's cheeks as she embraced Prince Meldiron. Holding the small prince was the only thing that seemed to calm her since her little boy had been so brutally taken from her.

Neirdre had aged since her mother had been killed, and Nestariel looked exhausted. Brijit imagined that she didn't look any better herself. After the attack, they had kept moving until they arrived at the settlement. Weylon had thought it too risky to make camp, and privately Brijit agreed with him. None of the others argued.

But traveling nonstop had taken its toll. They did have to rest the horses, but they had done so during the day and only for short periods of time. Weylon had always been watching the horizon, as had the two Elder soldiers with them.

The ramshackle settlement that lay out before them, really just a collection of rudimentary buildings, looked like heaven. Even Neirdre stopped complaining about the stench in the air when she realized that she would have a real bed to sleep in that night.

"We have the Elder princess and her newborn son," Weylon told Finn. "The Crown Prince sent us to you for safety."

Finn took in the tired-looking group and nodded. "Fair enough. That explains why this place has been fitted up as it has." He looked at Weylon. "I was questioning why there were so many supplies and rations when it was just me they sent out here."

He redirected his gaze to the group of women still huddled in the wagon. "Let's get you all settled. It looks like you could use some hot water and warm beds."

That was all Neirdre needed to hear to climb down from the wagon. Brijit followed her, stopping to help Aranel and Nestariel down. Finn came over and offered his arm to Nestariel when he saw the old Elder was a bit unsteady on her feet.

"Thank you, *Coimirceoirí*," she rasped. "It has been a long journey."

Finn nodded and directed them toward the large building in front of them. “There are beds for everyone. Come, get settled. I’ll let my people know that you are here.”

Brijit raised her eyebrows at that but then saw that there were, indeed, others milling around the building. A man and two boys ran forward to take the horses to the stable. There were several young girls hanging around a woman who appeared to be the housekeeper.

“Stella, tell Cook we have guests and they are going to need a hot meal and a good long night’s rest.”

The young red-haired girl nodded and then disappeared into the building.

Brijit smiled her thanks at Finn and then followed the others inside. She could hardly believe they were safe. She just hoped it lasted.

#

Weylon smiled at his friend. As the group milled around, Finn directed them to different rooms in the large building. Once they were all settled, he took Weylon into a common room and poured him a pint of ale.

Looking at his friend closely, he said, “Are you okay, Weylon?”

Weylon looked up, fear pricking his heart. Could Finn tell that easily that he had changed? Was the darkness so easy to see. “I’m fine,” he answered too sharply then quickly added, “Why?”

Finn narrowed his eyes at him. “You just…look different.” He shrugged and had a sip of his ale. “Probably you need a bath and a good rest.” Then he lowered his voice. “How bad was the journey here? The desert is rife with looters.”

Weylon nodded and told Finn about the attack. “We lost an old woman and a baby,” he said quietly, thanking the stars once again that the looter had chosen Aranel’s baby rather than the Crown Prince’s son. But then again, Brijit had been holding Meldiron. Weylon had arrived just as she took hold of that man’s mind, making him scream. He didn’t want to know what she had done to the criminal, but he was thankful she had protected the baby in her arms.

"And your fellow *Coimirceoirí*?" Finn asked.

Weylon stiffened, "What about her?" he asked coldly.

Finn chuckled. "That bad, eh?"

Weylon shook his head. He wasn't in the mood for Finn's riddles. "I don't know what you mean."

"Weylon, you were the one who always was saying not to get involved with our fellow *Coimirceoirí*! Now you've gone and done it."

He looked at Finn in surprise. "Why would you say that?"

"Because, my friend, if you didn't care about her an awful lot, you wouldn't be so angry." Finn held up his hand before Weylon could say anything. "And you, my friend, are angrier at that girl than I've ever seen you before."

"I have no feelings for her," Weylon said tonelessly. It was true. He didn't care about Brijit at all anymore, except for the low burn of hatred he felt for what she had done to him.

Finn just shook his head. "Okay, if that's what you say, buddy." Then he laughed quietly into his ale. "I really never thought I'd see the day when a girl would shake the concentration of the great Weylon Forborrow."

Weylon growled low in the throat and Finn got serious.

"I'm sorry. I'll stop. Where did they send you, Weylon?"

Weylon looked across the room unseeingly as the events of the last half-year played out in his memory. He looked at his friend who was watching him expectantly.

"It's a long story. I have much to tell you. But tonight the bed and bath you offered is calling to me."

Finn nodded. "And I have much to tell you as well, but you need to rest first."

Weylon finished his ale and stood.

Finn paused and then looked at his friend shrewdly.

"Oh, you should know something, Weylon."

Weylon smiled down at him. "What's that Finn?"

"I'm not the only one who is living in the Wastlands. We are not alone."

THE END

EAST SEA
Northlands
Pinefrest Mountains
Forbidden Coast
Pinefrest Forest
Green Lake
Western Realm
Glacier Field
Silvervale
Brindle
DarHills Mountains
DEAD SEA
The Rift
Revuover
Seremela
Eastern Mountains
Inn
Refuge
Lowlands
Gearmann
ACADEMY
Aranel Pallnen
Merryville
Outlands
Black Paw Mountains
Jirgen Forest
Bermgarten
Wastelands
Stone Mountain
Evendel
Southlands
Sallsburg
SEA OF ARCADIA

CPSIA information can be obtained
at www.ICGtesting.com
Printed in the USA
BVOW04s2028101216
470436BV00001B/21/P

9 781939 156877